Pra

LISA GRE

MY LIFE IN PINK & GREEN

"Displaying a lively familiarity with the topics of makeup, makeovers and adolescent angst, Greenwald makes a bright debut with this timely story." —*Publishers Weekly*

MY SUMMER OF PINK & GREEN

"Greenwald deftly blends eco-facts and makeup tips, friendship and family dynamics, and spot-on middle-school politics." —*Booklist*

PINK & GREEN IS THE NEW BLACK

"Greenwald's latest has an intimate, "girl to girl" feel that will resonate with those on the verge of teen (and tween)hood." —*School Library Journal*

AMULET BOOKS ★ NEW YORK

LISA GREENWALD

Welcome to Dog Beach

The Library of Congress has catalogued the
hardcover edition of this book as follows:
Greenwald, Lisa.
Welcome to Dog Beach / Lisa Greenwald.
pages cm
Summary: Eleven-year-old Remy loves the traditions of Seagate, the island where her family spends every summer vacation, but after her grandmother and a special dog dies, and her relationships with best friends Bennett and Micayla change, Remy takes comfort in the company of Dog Beach—where she hatches a plan to bring her friends closer and recapture the Seagate magic.
ISBN 978-1-4197-1018-6 (alk. paper)
[1. Summer—Fiction. 2. Vacations—Fiction. 3. Beaches—Fiction. 4. Friendship—Fiction. 5. Dogs—Fiction. 6. Dog walking—Fiction.] I. Title.
PZ7.G85199We 2014
[Fic]—dc23
2013023282

ISBN for this edition: 978-1-4197-1497-9

Printed and bound in U.S.A.
10 9 8 7 6 5 4 3 2 1

Amulet Books are available at special discounts when purchased in quantity for premiums and promotions as well as fundraising or educational use. Special editions can also be created to specification. For details, contact specialsales@abramsbooks.com or the address below.

THE ART OF BOOKS SINCE 1949
115 West 18th Street
New York, NY 10011
www.abramsbooks.com

For Aunt Emily, dog lover extraordinaire

And in memory of my beloved apricot poodle
Yoffi, the best dog in the history of dogs,
who I still believe may have been part human

On Seagate Island, there are three kinds of people: the lucky ones, the luckier ones, and the luckiest ones.

The lucky ones are the people who come for a weekend or maybe even a week. They stay at the Seagate Inn or they find a last-minute rental.

The luckier ones are the people who rent a house for the whole summer, Memorial Day to Labor Day. They usually come back summer after summer and stay in the same house.

And the luckiest ones are the people like me. I don't want to sound conceited—I'm grateful for how lucky I am. Because when it comes to Seagate Island, there's no doubt that I am the luckiest. I've spent every summer of my life on Seagate Island in my grandmother's house.

I was born at the end of May, so I spent my first three

months here. And I'll spend every summer here for the rest of my life. It's probably weird for me to think that far ahead, since I'm only eleven. But trust me—I will.

"Remy," I hear my mom calling from inside the house. I give her a few minutes to come outside and find me. It's kind of an unofficial house rule that if one of us is outside, the other one has to come out if they want to talk. No one should have to go inside to talk unless it's raining. On Seagate Island, our time outside by the sea is sacred. We've only been here for a week, and we have the whole summer stretched out in front of us, but we still don't take our outside time for granted.

I hear the quiet creak of the screen door, and then my mom pulls over the other wicker chair to sit next to me.

"Don't be mad, okay?" she asks, but it sounds more like a command than a question.

This can't be good.

"I just ran into Amber Seasons, and she's in a pickle," my mom starts. I wonder why people use the word *pickle* to mean a problem. In my mind, pickles are one of the most delicious foods. But I also get why people hate them. Bennett hates pickles. In fact, if he orders a hamburger and someone puts a pickle on his plate, he has to send the whole meal back. He feels bad about it, but he does it anyway. That's how much he hates pickles.

But Amber Seasons's being in a pickle isn't surprising. I've known her since I was born, pretty much, and she's always been in a pickle. She's fifteen years older than I am, and no matter what's going on, she always seems frazzled.

"What kind of pickle?" I ask.

"She offered to teach an art class for Seagate Seniors on Monday and Wednesday mornings at ten. But then her babysitter ended up staying in New Jersey for the summer, and now she needs someone to watch her son. She told me that's when he naps, so you'd just be sitting in her house every morning for a few hours."

I can't believe this is happening. This was going to be the first real summer that Micayla, Bennett, and I were allowed to roam free, all day, and do whatever we wanted.

In previous summers we were allowed to go off on our own, but only for a few hours at a time, and we needed to check in and always tell our parents where we were. But this summer was going to be different.

We're eleven now, going into sixth grade. That's middle school for Bennett and Micayla; it'll be the last year of elementary school for me.

And now I have to cut into that completely free time to watch Amber Seasons's son.

On the other hand, babysitting is kind of cool and something real teenagers do. I guess I'm older now and my mom thinks I'm more mature. I'm flattered that she thinks I can handle it.

"Please, Remy," my mom says. She's sitting on the wicker armchair with her head resting on her hands, and she looks pretty desperate. It's not even a favor for her, it's a favor for Amber Seasons, but I bet my mom already said that I'd do it. My mom has this weird thing about helping people solve their problems. She gets all jazzed up and has this intense, burning desire to help them, like she can't stop until she makes whatever situation they're in a little better. Helping other people makes her happier than anything else.

"Fine." I sigh, all defeated, but knowing I would never get out of it. "Maybe Micayla and Bennett can come with me some mornings?"

My mom considers that for a moment. "Well, you can certainly talk to Amber and ask her if it's okay."

She goes inside to finish getting ready for her afternoon swimming session, and I sit back in my chair and think. How bad will it really be? It's only a few hours two mornings a week.

My mom always says how good it makes her feel when she helps other people. So maybe I'll be like that too. I'll help Amber, and then I'll feel better. About everything.

Being sad on Seagate is kind of an oxymoron. The two things don't go together at all. But this year is different. I'm sad on Seagate, and I can't seem to help it.

"I got you two scoops," Micayla tells me when she walks through the house and finds me on the back porch. That's another thing about Seagate—no one locks their doors, and we all just barge into each other's homes. It can be awkward sometimes, like when I saw Bennett's mom getting out of the shower, but she had a towel on, and we just laughed about it. But the rest of the time it feels like the whole island's our home.

The turquoise ice cream cups from Sundae Best, Seagate Island's oldest and best ice cream shop, somehow make the ice cream taste even more delicious. I always get espresso cookie, and Micayla always gets cherry chip. When it comes to ice cream, we are as different as can be. But when it comes to almost everything else, we're pretty much the same.

Well, except that I'm white and she's black. And then there's also the difference of our hair—she wears it in braids year-round, and I have thin, straight, boring, not-quite-blonde and not-quite-brown hair that barely stays in an elastic band. Hers always looks good, even after she's just woken up.

Her parents are both from St. Lucia, in the Caribbean. They moved to the United States when they were kids but didn't meet until college. They have amazing accents, and when we're a little bit older, they're going to take me with them when they go back to visit Micayla's grandma in St. Lucia.

We take our ice cream cups and walk down the wooden stairs of my deck to the beach. Even though I do this at least ten times a day, I feel lucky every single time. On Seagate, the beach is my backyard, and I'm pretty sure there is nothing better than that in the whole world.

Sometimes we don't even bother with towels or chairs— we just sit down on the sand. We dig our feet in as far as they will go and we eat our ice cream. Our plan is to meet up with Bennett when he's done playing Ping-Pong with his dad, and then we'll decide what to do for the rest of the day.

"I hope this will cheer you up," Micayla says, burrowing through her ice cream cup for a chunk of chocolate. "I've never seen you sad on Seagate before."

She's right about that. But she's also never really seen me anywhere else, except for the time her dad brought her to New York City for a last-minute meeting. Her mom had flown to St. Lucia to visit Micayla's grandma, and Micayla couldn't stay home alone. So Micayla came to New York and we spent the day together. I don't think I was sad that day, so she's never really seen me sad anywhere, not just on Seagate. But I know what she means.

"I'm happy to be here. I just keep picturing Danish running on the beach . . . And his dog bed is still upstairs. I wish my parents would just throw it out, but I think they're too sad to do it. And the Pooch Parade during Seagate Halloween will be so horrible without him."

"I know," she says, not looking at me. "Well, maybe we can figure out something else to do during the Pooch Parade."

It's probably weird that it's not even July yet and I'm already thinking about Seagate Halloween, which takes place over Labor Day weekend. But it's one of the biggest traditions of the summer—everyone participates. Seagate Halloween is exactly the same every year, and that's the way I like it.

Bennett dresses up as Harvey from Sundae Best. He wears his shorts really high and a Seagate baseball cap. Micayla dresses up as a mermaid, like the statue you see when you first get off the ferry. I dress up as a beach pail. My mom makes me a new costume every year out of painted cardboard, and it comes out awesome every time. And the best part was that Danish would dress up as the shovel! We'd get the biggest sand shovel we could find and strap it to his back, and I'd carry him, so we looked like a perfect pair— beach pail and sand shovel. So happy together.

We've been on Seagate Island for a week, and I've been partially sad the whole time. Happy to be here, but sad without Danish. I don't want to be sad here. It's my most favorite place in the universe. But I can't seem to help it.

Danish was my grandma's dog, so for many years I only ever saw him on Seagate. Our house here was Grandma's house. When she died three years ago, we got Danish and the house, although it always seemed like they were partially ours to begin with.

During the summer, Danish slept in my bed. He spent all day with Micayla, Bennett, and me. Everyone thought he was my dog. And the house—well, the house felt like ours too. The yellow room with the canopy bed was mine. No one else slept there. Mom and Dad had the room around the corner with the blue-and-ivory-striped wallpaper. And Grandma's room was at the end of the hallway. She had her own bathroom, but she'd let us use it.

All year she'd be busy on Seagate, volunteering at the elementary school to help the kids with math, setting up the concert schedule for the summer, taking Danish to Dog Beach even when it was a little bit cold outside. Even though I knew all that, I always imagined her waiting patiently for us to come back for the summer. We'd come for weekends sometimes, but that didn't really count. Summer was summer.

Summer was when we were all together. Grandma would make her famous corn chowder. Mom would set up her easel on the back deck and paint landscapes of the ocean, and Dad would try to play Ping-Pong with everyone on the island at least once.

After Grandma died, we were all really sad. We couldn't imagine being on Seagate without her. But when we came back that next summer, being there was more comforting than we expected it to be. Everyone wanted to tell us stories about Grandma. Dad did some work on the house to spruce it up a little bit, and Mom organized a special concert in Grandma's memory. Now the annual concert series is known as the Sally Bell Seagate Concert Calendar.

Danish died this past December. It was sudden, and I don't really like to even think about it. All winter and spring, I kept hoping that being back on Seagate would be comforting, the way it was after Grandma died. But so far, it's not. So far, I just miss him. It was always Micayla, Bennett, and me—with Danish running along with us.

A key member of our crew is missing.

"I have to tell you something," Micayla and I say at the exact same time, and then we both burst into laughter.

"You first," I say. She probably has more exciting news than my babysitting job.

"Avery Sanders has a boyfriend," Micayla tells me.

"Yeah?" I ask. "She didn't mention it to me when I saw her at Pastrami on Rye the other night."

"Just saw her at Sundae Best. She was going on and on about it. She said this new kid moved to Seagate in the middle of the year. And he's, like, a real-life boyfriend."

I look at Micayla, surprised. "I wonder why she didn't tell me before."

Avery Sanders is a friend of ours, but not a best friend. She moved to Seagate four years ago, and she lives here year-round. She's the type of friend that we never really call to make plans, but if we run into each other, we'll hang out.

She's nice, but she's one of those girls who seemed like a teenager when we were, like, nine, and she'd always say that Bennett was my boyfriend, even when I didn't really know what a boyfriend was.

The past few times I talked to her, she told me that she was bored with Seagate and that it has really changed since she moved here.

I always listened to what she said, even though none of it made sense. How could Seagate be boring? And how could it change? Seagate will always be perfect, and summer after summer, it always stays the same. That's the beauty of it.

"I think her grandparents live here year-round now too," Micayla tells me. "That's what my mom said."

Actually, that's another group of lucky people on Seagate—the year-rounders. I always wonder if that makes them luckier than the luckiest or somewhere in between. On the one hand, they never have to leave Seagate. But on the other hand, they have to see almost everyone else leave. And they don't get that amazing anticipation—the excited, heart-bursting feeling of coming back.

"What did you have to tell me?" Micayla asks.

I explain the whole pickle situation with Amber Seasons.

"That's cool," Micayla says. "It's, like, your first real job."

"You think?"

"Yeah, for sure." She digs deep in her cup for the last little bit of ice cream. "And it's only a few hours. You won't miss anything."

"I guess."

Micayla gives me her please-cheer-up smile again and taps my leg. "Come on. Let's go meet Bennett at Ping-Pong. Bennett always makes you laugh after five minutes."

She's right about that.

"Who's he playing?" I ask Micayla as we get closer to the stadium. It's not really a stadium, but since Ping-Pong is such a huge deal on Seagate Island, that's what we call it. It's really just a big overhang in the middle of the island with fifteen Ping-Pong tables underneath it. This way people can play rain or shine.

"He said he was meeting his dad here. You know they take their Sunday games really seriously."

Bennett's dad only comes to Seagate on the weekends. He's a big lawyer in Boston. He flies in every Friday and flies back every Sunday on these teeny-tiny planes. Bennett and his dad always have a heated Ping-Pong match right before he leaves on Sunday afternoon. Bennett usually wins.

"Remy! Mic!" Bennett shouts to us. "Where have you guys been?"

We walk closer to his table and see that he's playing against a kid with spiky hair and a shirt with a picture of a video game controller on it.

"Yo, Calvin." Bennett turns to the spiky-haired kid. He's really not the type of person to use the word *yo*, so hearing him say it is strange. "This is Remy." Bennett points to me. "And this is Micayla." He points to her.

"Hey," Calvin says, looking down at his untied sneakers like he doesn't really care to talk to us. We say "hey" back, and then Bennett and Calvin return to their game.

There's a girl sitting on one of the wooden benches along the side of the stadium. "Calvin, come on," she says. "Grandpa said we needed to be back by three."

"Claire." He keeps playing and doesn't look at her. "Shut up."

"Calvin!" The girl yells this time. "Fine. Whatever. I'm leaving you here. I hope you get lost."

I guess she doesn't realize that it's pretty much impossible to be lost on Seagate.

She huffs, annoyed, as she stands up and walks away. She doesn't introduce herself to us, and she doesn't say good-bye to Bennett. She's wearing white cutoffs, and they're really, really short, so she adjusts them as she walks away.

"My sister is such a bore," Calvin says.

"Most girls are," Bennett replies.

What did he just say? I look at Micayla to see if she heard it, but she's more involved in their game than I realized. Bennett Newhouse, one of my best friends since birth, just said that most girls are bores. At least he said "most" and not "all," but *still.*

Finally Calvin leaves and Bennett walks over to Micayla and me. "Surfing?" he asks. As much as I want to go surf, I'm still kind of shaken up. If he thinks most girls are bores, does he think I'm a bore? Or does he not think of me as a girl?

"There will be time for surfing after we discuss what just happened," I tell Bennett. Micayla cracks up. She says that I speak in a really formal way because both of my parents are on-air journalists. She tells me I should talk more like a kid. I think I talk like a kid most of the time, but my more formal speech comes out when I'm angry. Like I am right now. "Why did you say that girls are bores?"

"Uh-oh, Investigator Remy is here again!" Bennett laughs and raises a hand to slap Micayla five, but she denies him. "Rem, relax. I just met the kid. I was trying to make him feel comfortable."

I give him a casual eye roll. That's a lame excuse if I ever heard one. "Well, who is he anyway? A weekender?"

Bennett shuffles some stray sand around with the toe of his flip-flop. "No. He's my next-door neighbor."

"What?" Micayla exclaims. "What happened to Mr. Brook-field?"

"That's his grandson! The one he was always telling us about." Bennett widens his eyes at us, and I can't tell if he wants us to be excited or not. "Remember?"

"Kind of." I shrug. I do remember, but I don't want to admit it; I'm still mad at Bennett. Mr. Brookfield always went on and on about his grandchildren and how we'd love them if we only knew them. But they always went to camp in the summer and had no interest in Seagate.

That was okay with me. I already had friends, and while people say you can never have too many, I was happy with the way things had always been.

"That girl was his twin, then," I say, putting it all together. "Didn't Mr. Brookfield always say he had twin grandchildren?"

"Yup. Calvin and Claire."

Calvin and Claire—sounds like a matched pair. I decide that I'll think of them as the C Twins.

"Please tell me they're just here for the week," Micayla says, and I'm glad she does, because that means I don't have to. "July Fourth week and then they're going home?"

"Nope. They'll be here all summer." Bennett raises his eyebrows, like he's not sure why this is such a big deal. "So? Surfing?"

"Why are they here?" I ask.

Micayla chimes in, "Yeah. I thought they loooved camp."

It's not that we don't believe camp can be great. I go to school with a girl named Rachel Kleiger who claims camp is the best place on earth. She feels about camp the way I feel about Seagate. But we just never understood how these twins could choose a camp over Seagate. Seagate is perfect.

And anyone who has an option to be here should be here.

"I don't know, guys," Bennett says. "I just met them today." He backs up a little bit. "You're both acting weird. I'm going to surf."

Micayla and I hang back a minute and tell Bennett that we'll meet him at the beach. After he leaves, I say, "*We're* acting weird? *He's* acting weird." I look at Micayla and wait for her to say something. "Right?"

She shrugs. I wish she'd agree with me more. "I'm still thinking about that kid Calvin's hair. It was unusual, right?"

"I forgot what it looked like already," I lie. I don't know why I lie, but I do.

"Brown and spiky?" I can't believe Micayla just believed me.

"Oh yeah. That's not really so unusual."

On the way back to the beach we pick up our surfboards and change into our bathing suits. They're still wet from our morning swim, but we don't mind. They're just going to get wet again anyway. On Seagate, it's okay to walk around in a damp bathing suit. No one judges you. There's no pressure to show off. I feel kind of guilty that I'm so judgy about Calvin and his sister. Maybe they're not that bad.

Maybe it's just that I'm still feeling off. Things are different. Without Danish, I can't seem to get into the summer groove. Add to that Bennett's weird comment, and Micayla being so focused on their game and Calvin's hair. Everything seems a little strange.

I decide to put it all out of my head and try to stop thinking for just a minute. Micayla and I run into the sea holding hands like we always do. We like to swim for a few minutes before we attempt to surf. It's kind of like how the Olympic divers go into that hot tub before they dive, or runners stretch before a race.

We need to warm up.

Maybe that's kind of how it is with summer too. You have to get back into the swing of things. I decide that this past week has been my warm-up week, my few minutes in the ocean before surfing.

Everyone needs time to adjust. Even on Seagate. Even me.

Danish was a miniature poodle. He had apricot fur and weighed thirteen pounds, and he acted more like a human than a dog. He also had expensive taste. One time, for my cousin's bar mitzvah, we had to stay at a motel in Toronto. It was an okay place, but Danish hated it there. He barked the whole time. We had to take him to the bar mitzvah party because the other hotel guests were so sick of his barking! At the party, he sat at the table with us and even won the limbo competition.

Then, a few months later, we traveled to Washington, DC, for my mom's friend's wedding, and we stayed at a real hotel with a pool and a ballroom and everything. It was way fancier, and Danish loved it. They gave him special dog treats and had a dog sitter come and walk him while we were at the wedding. He didn't even care that we left and didn't bark once. We were treated like celebrities there, and Danish knew it.

Danish liked going for walks, but he preferred to sit with us on the couch while we watched TV. He ate his meals when we ate our meals. His food bowl and water bowl sat on a mat beside our kitchen table. When he was done eating, he'd hop up onto his bench near the kitchen window and wait for us to finish.

After Grandma died, my mom bought that bench just for Danish. It's antique, with a gold velvet cushion and brass finishes, and it was the perfect width for Danish. Most people don't buy human furniture specifically for their dogs. But Danish had human tastes, and we did what made him happy.

Danish adjusted to life in Manhattan, but he was happiest on Seagate, just like all of us. He could roam free there, like I could, and he didn't really need a leash anyway—he always stayed right by my side.

This is going to sound crazy and it doesn't make any sense, but I always believed Danish would live forever. We read that book *Tuck Everlasting* last year in school, and so I'd tell myself that Danish drank the magic potion, just like Jesse. And that Danish and I would always be together.

I guess most of me knew that was totally made up and that no one lives forever—but a tiny part of me believed it anyway.

I wait a moment, wipe my tears, and take a deep breath before I go into Amber Seasons's house. It's my first day of work, and I don't want to look like a complete basket case. Her son'll be napping, but I still need to seem professional. At least that's what my mom said.

I'll be okay eventually. I know that. I asked the vet, Dr. Laterno, how long people usually feel sad after their dog dies, and she said it depends. That everyone is different. I just wanted a set answer. Like, six weeks and you'll feel much better. Or even six months. Just so I knew what I'd be dealing with. But I guess it doesn't work that way.

"Remy, I can't thank you enough," Amber says as she opens the door to let me in. "You're a lifesaver. Hudson is upstairs sleeping, and he'll probably nap the whole time I'm out. I was lucky to get a good sleeper." She says the last part under her breath.

I nod. Don't people say that "they slept like a baby" when they've had a good night's sleep? I thought that meant that all babies slept well.

"My girl is the difficult one," she continues.

"You have two kids?" I ask. "My mom only mentioned one."

"Oh, no." She laughs. "I have one kid and one dog. I refer to her as my girl." Right then a little Yorkie comes running in. "This is my darling, Marilyn Monroe. But ever since Hudson was born, she's become ultra-feisty and jealous and, let's face it, pretty demanding."

I nod, slowly, trying to see what she's talking about. But all I observe is an adorable little Yorkie with a hot pink bow on her head. She jumps up as high as my knee and wags her tail, and when I pet her, I swear she smiles. A smiling dog! Danish was a smiler too, though I think I was the only one who could really see it.

"So Hudson will be asleep, but if you can give Mari a little attention, that would be amazing." She smiles and gives me a hug. "You're the best, Remy."

A few minutes later, Amber is out the door carrying an easel and a coffee can of paintbrushes. I quickly tiptoe upstairs and put my ear to the door of Hudson's room. Nothing. Good.

I tiptoe back downstairs and make myself comfortable on Amber's gray burlap couch. I take a copy of *Ocean Living* magazine off the coffee table, but before I even pull back the front cover, I hear the jingling of Marilyn Monroe's tags and she jumps up onto the couch and starts licking my face like I'm her new favorite person in the world.

"I'm happy to see you too, Marilyn Monroe."

She licks me even more and then settles down, sitting so close to me that one of her paws rests on my leg.

I try to go back to reading, but it's difficult because Marilyn Monroe is just sitting there, staring at me, as if she's asking me, "What's next?" or "What are we going to do now?" So I put down the magazine and look back at her.

"I used to have a dog," I start. And I tell her all about Danish. She barks at just the right spots, like she understands me and gets what I'm saying. And when I tell her that Danish died this past winter, she lets out a little whimper.

"You're sweet, Marilyn Monroe," I say. "Thanks for listening." She licks my hand, as if to say she's always here to listen. For some reason, she's the easiest person to talk to. Okay, I know she's not a person. Easiest creature to talk to?

I wonder why that is. I never had trouble talking to Micayla before, but I haven't told her all this stuff about Danish and how I'm feeling. Maybe it's gotten harder for some reason.

"If I had known you'd be here, I wouldn't have been so grumbly about taking this job." She looks at me, head tilted. "Don't tell Amber I said that. Or Hudson."

She lets out a little yelp, and I'm pretty sure my secret is safe with her.

I'm surprised when Amber shows up just a little bit later. It feels like she's only been gone ten minutes, but I look at the clock, and it's noon. Hudson's still asleep, and Marilyn Monroe is sipping some water out of her bowl, dainty and delicate, not getting any on the floor and very little on her face.

Amber thanks me again and again, and I tell her it was no trouble, but in my head, I'm wondering if I'm the one who should be thanking her.

Micayla has a theory that avoiding Dog Beach is making me sadder about Danish.

"Let's just go there. It's your favorite place, and turning away every time we walk by isn't helping," she says one morning.

Dog Beach is pretty crowded for only eleven in the morning. It's at the farthest end of Seagate, but since Seagate is a pretty small island, nothing is really that far from anything else. With unobstructed views of the ocean and the signature Seagate white fencing, Dog Beach is one of the prettiest places on the island. Even non-dog-owners think so.

I look around at all the dogs, and I'm not sure Micayla's theory is right. I'm sad all over again. Danish's friend Cookie the beagle is here, and Palm the Pomeranian. Palm's owners live on Seagate half the year, and West Palm Beach, Florida, the other half, so that's why they named him Palm. Most of Danish's friends were little dogs, but his best friend was a Dalmatian named Hampton. They were an odd pair, one so big and one so little, but they'd play together and look out for each other. And now Hampton's here on his own, off to the side playing with a yellow Lab. Must be a newcomer. I get a scraped-knee stinging feeling that maybe Danish has been replaced.

In a way, Hampton and Danish kind of reminded me of Bennett and me. Hampton was outgoing and boisterous while Danish was quiet, taking everything in. But they got along so well.

The dogs on Seagate are like the people—you can tell which ones are here for a week for the first time and which ones will be here until August, like they are every summer.

"Aren't you glad to be here?" Micayla asks, tying her braids into a low ponytail. "Let's go sit on one of the benches and people- and dog-watch. I'm too hot to stand up."

I nod. "Are you sure you're okay? You're not going to have some crazy allergic attack?"

Micayla is seriously allergic to dogs that shed, but she loves them anyway. She can't resist petting them, and then she gets all sneezy and her eyes turn red and watery and she complains a lot. But she still loves them.

"Of course, I'm fine." She smiles.

Bennett goes to play with the dogs. He picks up one of the extra Frisbees and starts playing fetch with a golden retriever. Bennett's a dog person even though his family has never had one.

The golden retriever's owner (who must be a newcomer, since I don't recognize her) comes over to play too. She looks like she's around forty, but I can see Bennett saying something that's making her laugh.

Bennett can talk to anyone. It doesn't matter how old they are, if they're a girl or a boy, even if they're human, really. I just saw him talking to that golden retriever. He called out, "Mickey, here boy!" just like he'd been friends with that dog for years.

While we're watching the dogs and Bennett play, I tell Micayla about Marilyn Monroe and how we had a pretty awesome time together.

"Is she here now?" Micayla asks.

"No, I don't see her." I admit—I'm a little disappointed. I was sort of hoping she'd be here.

"Well, she can be, like, your almost-dog this summer," Micayla says. "Do you think your parents will want to get another dog one day?"

"I doubt it. A dog isn't like a new pair of flip-flops that you can just replace," I tell her. "It takes time."

"I know," she says. "I mean, I don't know, because I've never had a dog, but I know you can't just trade one for another."

Micayla links arms with me even though we're still sitting on the bench. "Come on, let's walk and look at the dogs."

We spend the next hour playing with a pair of Malteses named Snowball and Marshmallow. They're puppies, and the Howells just got them. The Howells are an older couple who live on the other side of the island. We always see them at the deli, Pastrami on Rye. My mom always jokes that they don't even need a kitchen since it seems that they eat every meal there.

"How are you, Remy?" Mrs. Howell asks.

"Good," I reply. "Happy to be back on Seagate." I usually answer this way. I wish I had more to say, but nothing seems to come to mind. I used to be so good at talking to adults, but now I get nervous. I'm not sure why.

"Us too," Mrs. Howell says. "And these guys are so happy to be here. They were running in circles in our Brooklyn apartment. That hasn't been fun for any of us."

Snowball keeps jumping up on my legs and licking my knees, and it makes me laugh.

"She likes you, Rem," Micayla tells me.

The two white fluff balls keep jumping on us, and I love watching them. But they're not my dogs, and eventually we have to leave them behind. Micayla and I wave good-bye to Bennett, who says he'll catch up with us at my house, and we start walking home.

"It's settled," Micayla says. "You're amazing with dogs, and you're going to be a vet when you grow up."

"I don't know, Mic," I say. "But I'm glad I have you as my cheerleader."

"Speaking of cheerleaders," she says, kicking a rock along the path, "did you hear that Seagate is getting a basketball team this year? Avery Sanders told me, of course. Her boyfriend can't wait to try out."

"I didn't hear that." To be honest, I never think about the school here. I don't like to think about kids being here when I'm not. Maybe that's really selfish of me. But Seagate feels like a summer-only place sometimes.

"Yeah, for seventh and eighth graders."

"But who would they play? They'd have to take the bridge or the ferry for any matches." There's only one school on Seagate. It goes from kindergarten to eighth grade, and after that the kids have to go off the island for high school. It's only about a twenty-minute ferry ride or a quick drive over the bridge. It's not a big deal, but it's very different from what I'm used to. Back home in New York, I can walk to my school, and when I'm in high school, I'll probably take the subway. You're always connected when you've got a subway.

"Yeah, they play the other schools in Ferry Port and Seaside, I guess."

Micayla doesn't say much after that, and when we get to my house, my parents are sitting on the back porch reading the newspaper and drinking pink lemonade. They're both here for all of July, and then when August comes they take turns going back and forth to the city. When Grandma was here, they would go to the city more often, but even though I'm allowed to be alone a lot of the time, I can't stay alone overnight.

"Hi, girls," my mom says in her cheerful Seagate voice. I call it her Seagate voice because I rarely hear it in New York City. Back in New York, she's stressed and frazzled. She complains about people who honk too much, people who push on the subway, her boss, and how much everything costs. But on Seagate, that fades away. It's all painting and reading the newspaper and walks on the beach.

"Hi," I say. "Micayla's mom invited me to go for fish sandwiches with them tonight. Can I go?"

"No interest in my famous salmon casserole?" my dad asks. "Micayla?"

He always asks this, even though he knows the answer. I think that's why he asks, because he likes to see how we'll respond. Micayla always tries to be super polite and give a reasonable answer for why she can't eat it. He's been asking this same question for years, but she's still polite. That says something about her, I think.

"Well, I would, but my parents have been talking about fish sandwiches for days, and now I'm really craving one," she says. "But thanks anyway."

Super polite. Always. That's my best friend Micayla.

"Okay, okay. I'll try not to cry," my dad says. "Good thing Abby likes it."

My mom rolls her eyes. "Oh, I love it."

My dad's salmon casserole is one of the only things he can make, and it's his favorite. He tries really hard and adds new touches to it all the time, like green peppers and bread crumbs. But it's really just a mishmash of canned salmon, mayonnaise, spiral pasta, and random stuff he finds around the house. It kind of gives me a stomachache when I think about it. But my dad really wants us to like it, so we try to pretend that we do.

"So, Mr. and Mrs. Boltuck, how's the summer going?" Micayla starts, sitting next to my mom on the wicker love seat.

"Micayla, please." My mom smiles. "Call us Abby and Reed."

"Okay. Do-over." Micayla laughs. "Abby and Reed, how's the summer going?"

We sit around chatting, waiting for Bennett to show up, and then we'll walk over to Frederick's Fish together.

Micayla's telling us this story about how her dad's computer crashed and he lost the whole draft of the biography he's working on when I hear the creak of the screen door. I turn around and see Bennett running through the house. He bursts out onto the back deck. "Am I late? I'm so sorry. Little Jakey Steinman lured me in for a game of Ping-Pong. You know those six-year-olds. You can't say no. And he plays a mean game."

"Hi, Bennett," my dad says. "Have a seat."

Bennett sits way back in the chair, and it almost falls over. He makes this weird face, and Micayla and I crack up.

"You guys seem like you're up to no good," my dad says.

"Huh?" I ask.

"We were just at Dog Beach," Bennett says. "It's kind of like Remy's therapy. We think it will help her feel better about Danish."

My dad nods, then grins like he's going to say something funny—but I know from experience it won't be funny. At all. "Got it. For a second, I thought you and Remy were eloping!"

"Dad!" I yell. And even though he's made this joke a million times, it feels different this summer. I want to sink into the indentation in the middle of my lounge chair and bury myself in the sand. I can't look at my dad and I can't look at Bennett. All I can see is the wicker ottoman in the corner, the one that Danish liked to use for sunbathing. And then my sadness wipes away my embarrassment.

I'm not sure which feeling is worse.

People have been making jokes about Bennett and me getting married since we were tiny babies. His birthday is the day after mine. Apparently we were both terrible newborns, and we both spent our first summers on Seagate. His mom met my mom at a Seagate new mothers group, and they became best friends immediately.

They say we were the worst babies on the whole island, and they were so glad they found each other so that they could commiserate.

There are pictures of us as babies in sun tents on the beach, sleeping in our strollers side by side as our dads played Ping-Pong. Summer after summer, as we got older, the pictures evolved. They morphed into us trying to eat soft-serve in cones, the ice cream melting all over our faces, and of us burying each other in the sand or wearing different homemade costumes at the annual Seagate Halloween Parade.

We never really paid much attention to these jokes when Avery Sanders said them, or my dad or Bennett's dad or anyone else. But it feels different now. I just wish people would stop saying it.

My dad puts his feet up on the ottoman and looks at his watch. "Well, if you three are going for fish sandwiches, you'd better skedaddle."

He's right. It's a little after five and Frederick's Fish always gets lines for dinner. Micayla's brother and sister are here this week, so we'll be a big group.

Micayla, Bennett, and I walk over to Frederick's Fish, dragging our feet a little, not talking much.

"You seem better today," Micayla says, as we walk past SGI Sweets, Seagate's famous candy store. "I mean, not your usual Seagate happy, but better than you've been."

"I guess." When I hear myself say it, I can tell I'm acting like a downer. I should be more appreciative to Micayla for being so supportive. "Let's go into SGI," I tell her. "I want to buy you some of those gummy apples."

She doesn't argue with me. I knew she wouldn't. They're her absolute favorite candy, and they're impossible to find anywhere but Seagate. We buy a big bag and share them as we walk.

At the fish place, Micayla's family is already waiting in line. Her mom is sitting on one of the benches, and her dad, brother, and sister are standing a few feet away. They're smiling, but as we get closer, it seems that they're talking about something important—they're leaning in and speaking quietly. Micayla's mom is not a part of the conversation, and she seems to be daydreaming a little bit. We have to tap her a few times before she realizes that we're there.

"Are Zane and Ivy staying the whole week?" Micayla asks her mom.

When her mom replies, "I'm not sure yet," I start to get the feeling that something weird is going on. Micayla's mom is a super planner and she always knows what's going on—today, three weeks away, even a year from now.

I start to wonder why Bennett and I were invited to this family dinner. Even though we always do everything together, we usually have some separate family time. It's expected that there will be some nights when we're each with our own family; no one gets mad about it.

But as the meal goes on, no one says anything to explain the weird feeling in the air. I wonder if Bennett notices it too. Ivy and Zane make jokes about the new Seagate basketball team, and Micayla's dad talks about the biography he's working on about Franklin D. Roosevelt. Micayla's mom asks us questions about the other kids on Seagate and if the new salted caramel flavor at Sundae Best is as good as everyone says it is.

I keep sensing that something unusual is going on, but I have no idea what it is.

Good thing the fish sandwiches at Frederick's are as delicious as always, because when the food comes, eating it up is all I can think about.

A few mornings later, I wake up to a text from Bennett saying that he and Micayla are going to get egg-and-cheese sandwiches at Breakfast by the Boardwalk and that I should meet them there.

They get up much earlier than I do, so they usually don't text me until at least nine in the morning. When I look at the seashell clock above my doorway, I see that it's already close to ten. The text message came in at exactly nine, and I doubt they're still there. I sleep later on the mornings I'm not babysitting Hudson and hanging out with Marilyn Monroe.

When I text him back, he says that they already finished eating and that they're over at Mr. Brookfield's house and that I should come over.

I haven't seen the C Twins since the other day at Ping-Pong, and I'd nearly forgotten about them.

My parents are down by the community pool when I tell them I'm heading out. They look up from their books and tell me to have fun.

I'm wearing my yellow halter one-piece under my rainbow cover-up, and I realize it's the first time I've walked alone on Seagate since we got here. Normally I'm with Bennett or Micayla or both. And in the past, I never walked alone. I always had Danish with me.

I ring the doorbell to Mr. Brookfield's. I hardly ever ring doorbells on Seagate, but I don't know Mr. Brookfield well enough to just barge right in. He greets me at the door with a "howdy" and tells me how much taller I've gotten since last summer. I never know what to say to this, so I just smile.

"The gang's in the back," he tells me.

I'm on my way there when I hear the screaming. It startles me so much that I jump back a few feet and knock over one of Mr. Brookfield's porcelain director's chairs. He has them all over the house—miniature ones, wooden ones, metal ones, even a few large enough to sit on. Bennett told us that he was a movie fanatic, and when we'd visit before, we were always super careful not to break any of them.

I hear the screaming again, and I try to figure out who it is. Bennett never screams like that. It's definitely not Micayla. Claire is super girly and dainty—at least that's how she seemed the other day. Calvin? I can't figure out why he'd be screaming so loud.

It's not like any old scream, like during a fight or when

someone's scared, or even when they drop a mug accidentally. It's a high-powered scream, almost like in a cartoon, but realistic, like it's coming from a regular person.

On Seagate, nothing all that scary happens, so no one really screams. There aren't any mice or rats—at least, I haven't seen any, thank God. There's no armed robbery or mugging. There's the occasional ocean rescue, when a little kid goes out too far, but they're always rescued right away. The lifeguards on Seagate are the best in the world. That's what my mom says.

I look around, wondering why Mr. Brookfield hasn't come running out. When I finally spot him, he's just sitting in his sunroom reading a magazine. I guess he's not worried that someone is screaming really loudly in his backyard, so I try not to worry about it either and head back.

Bennett, Micayla, and the C Twins sit crouched around a little tape player. My grandma used to have one of them, but we got rid of it after she died. We didn't even own any cassette tapes, so there was no reason to own a player.

"Rem, come listen to this," Bennett yells to me. "You're never going to believe it."

I walk down the few steps from the deck to the backyard but stop when I hear Rae and Rudy Spitz bickering. They've been married for more than sixty years, but we never see them talking nicely to each other, only fighting. We figure that's just how they communicate.

"I told you thirty times to water those flowers!" Rae yells.

"All right, all right. Enough."

"Don't *enough* me, Rudy!"

"Rae! You're making me crazy!"

"Those Spitzes!" Calvin says under his breath, cracking up. "We've heard my grandfather say that a million times already, and we've only been here a few days."

"I don't know how he's lived next door to them all these years," Claire says, looking unimpressed and sort of bored with the conversation. "Oh. Hi, Remy."

"Hi," I say back to be nice. Claire's one of those girls who always seems to be bothered. It could be the weather or the way her sneakers fit or that she's not allowed to have dessert, but it's always something. I've only known her for a few days, but that type of thing is really obvious.

"Rem, come here," Bennett says again, and I finally make my way to the tape player. "You gotta hear this."

He presses Play and I hear that scream, the one I heard just a few minutes ago. It sounded so clear and lifelike that I had no idea it was a recording. Bennett then proceeds to play it ten more times. He seems so interested in it that I can't help but be interested in it too.

When Bennett gets enthusiastic about something, I automatically want to know more about it. He just has this way of making even everyday things seem more interesting.

"Okay, whoa," I say, laughing. "That's a lot of screaming. Explain?"

I don't know how it's possible for a scream to sound so

incredible, but this one does. There's something almost magical about it.

Bennett turns to Calvin and Claire, who are eating a sleeve of Chips Ahoy like they haven't seen food in years. "You guys want to tell the story?" he asks them.

Micayla reaches in for a cookie and shrugs. "I don't really know what's going on either," she whispers to me.

Calvin sighs and plops down on the grass. He puts his baseball cap across his face like he needs a second to regain his concentration, and then he says, "Our grandfather is that scream."

I've known Mr. Brookfield forever, and he's always been the nice older man who lives next door to Bennett's family. He was friends with my grandma. He likes to walk around Seagate and pick up any trash, even though that's not a huge job because no one really litters here. He also plays cards down by the Ping-Pong stadium and was a judge for the Sandcastle Contest a few times. But that's really all I know about him.

I've never heard him raise his voice. I have no idea what Calvin means when he says that Mr. Brookfield "is that scream."

Claire's pulling up grass to make bracelets, but she chimes in, "His scream has been in a million movies." She rolls her eyes. "But he has no connections. I really wanted to meet someone famous, but he says he can't do anything."

"Mr. Brookfield is famous?" I look at Bennett when I ask

this because I feel uncomfortable talking to Claire, and Calvin doesn't really make much sense.

"Well, no. I mean, um, he's not, right?" Bennett asks Calvin. "I think he should be, though."

"He doesn't even really seem to care," Calvin says, twirling a finger beside his head, the universal sign for cuckoo. I can't believe Calvin and Claire talk about their own grandfather, sweet Mr. Brookfield, this way.

"Wait," Micayla says, crumpling up the empty sleeve of cookies. "Why isn't he famous if his scream was in a million movies? I'm so confused."

Claire looks up at the sky, as if searching for some kind of divine help to get her out of this annoying situation. "Basically they just paid him to record the scream once, but it's been in, like, billions of movies, and no one knows it's him. I swear, if you watch movies like *Star Wars* and *Indiana Jones* and even some Disney cartoons, you'll hear it."

"That's really cool and kind of crazy," I say, making eye contact with Bennett, hoping he realizes that I think it's cool too. I could tell Bennett was all excited about it, but Claire and Calvin act like it's no big deal.

"You guys don't get it. It would be cool if he was actually, like, famous," Claire says. "But he's *not*."

Claire has to be the most negative person on Seagate. She doesn't belong here. She belongs in New York City on the hottest day of the year, on garbage pickup day; that way she'd be able to find a million more negative people.

I keep thinking about the Scream, and as cool as it is, it also kind of freaks me out. How can I have lived near Mr. Brookfield for so long and never known this about him? It makes me feel nervous.

"So why are you on Seagate this summer anyway?" Micayla asks Claire.

"We were forced to come," Claire says. "Grandpa's getting older and our parents want us to spend time with him."

"We love the guy, but no offense, it's kind of slow here." Calvin widens his eyes at us. "And the guy may be getting weirder; he's talking about his scream more, which only makes me think he's going crazy."

He did *not* just say what I thought he did. Newcomers talking badly about our beloved Seagate? I want to get up and walk away and not talk to these two ever again. If it's slow here, it's because *they're* boring. They obviously don't get the magic of this place, and I don't really care to show it to them.

Besides, is revealing a secret really a sign of someone going crazy? I don't think so. Plus, I don't want that to be true. Even though Bennett thinks it's awesome, part of me hopes Mr. Brookfield will stop talking about this weird scream and go back to being the nice old man who picks up any litter he sees—this changes everything about him.

"Well, if you think it's slow here, you'll just have to hang with us," Bennett says. "We'll show you how awesome it is."

I literally feel my mouth dropping open like an exaggerated cartoon character. I look at Micayla to commiserate, but she seems distracted, ripping the strands of her cutoffs. She doesn't seem to understand what a serious disaster has occurred.

Bennett Newhouse, one of my best friends in the entire world, just invited these two downers to hang with us.

The worst part is, they still don't seem happy. Claire goes on and on about the celebrities she'd like to meet if only her grandfather was famous enough to actually help her meet them, and Calvin just plays with his hat.

It occurs to me that instead of sitting around talking about celebrities we're never going to meet, we could go inside and ask Mr. Brookfield about the Scream and get him to tell us why he kept it a secret all these years. It explains his director's chair collection, for one thing. But I also want to ask him how it happened, and what it was like to be in the movies, and if he ever screams to himself every now and again.

He has this mystery past. Everyone just sees him as nice Mr. Brookfield, but there's actually so much more to him, and hardly anyone even knows about it. Only us.

I start to get the feeling that maybe that's true for everyone. Maybe all grown-ups have mystery pasts, and it takes random old artifacts to discover what they are. Maybe kids have the same thing. Not mystery pasts, but secret feelings. Only a few people know how sad I am about Danish. I just carry it around with me like an oversized backpack, one that's invisible to pretty much everyone.

I think about all of this as the rest of the group goes on and on about what it's like to be famous.

When there's a lull in the conversation, I suggest we go for a swim. It's getting really hot out here. And underwater, I can think all I want about secret lives, and I don't have to listen to the C Twins at all.

Micayla and her mom are going to get their hair rebraided this morning. I've gone with them a few times, and it's cool, but it takes a really long time.

Bennett's mom is taking him and his little brother, Asher, on a fishing expedition. If Danish were here, we'd go for an early-morning stroll along the beach and then stop at Daisy's for pancakes on the way home. Daisy's is a restaurant for humans and canines. That's what the sign says. Daisy McDougal is a dog lover through and through, and so she set up a little doggie eating area on the porch of her restaurant. There are bowls of water and buckets of treats for the dogs.

It's one of my favorite places on Seagate. I've been avoiding it this summer for obvious reasons.

So instead of pancakes, I decide to smear some cream cheese on a bagel and head over to Marilyn Monroe's. I know it's Amber's house and I'm really there to watch her son, but after just a few mornings together, it seems that my main purpose is to spend time with Marilyn Monroe. And I'm okay with that.

"Oh, what a morning!" Amber says as soon as she sees me. "My personal trainer canceled my afternoon appointment, and Marilyn Monroe was craving a trip to Daisy's—I could tell. But we never made it out for our morning walk."

"That sounds . . . stressful," I say. Sometimes it's hard for me to really understand what she's worried about.

"But Hudson is down, finally, and Marilyn Monroe was somewhat satisfied with a few extra treats," she tells me. "Thanks again, Remy."

"No problem," I say. "And . . . um . . . I could take Marilyn Monroe to Daisy's later, I mean, if you want."

"You'd do that?" she asks. "She can be a handful. She never quite got the hang of walking on a leash, heeling, and all that."

"I can handle it," I say. "I mean, if you want. We can talk about it when you get back. I don't want you to be late."

"You're the best, Remy." Amber grabs all her supplies and her iced coffee and heads out for the art class.

"I love Daisy's too," I tell Mari when we're settled and cozy on the couch. "I understand how you feel."

She does her little "I agree" yelp, and we settle back into the couch for our usual morning chatting session.

"I went to Dog Beach finally," I tell her. "I had been avoiding it, but my friends dragged me there. You haven't met them yet—Micayla and Bennett—but they're pretty awesome."

She looks up at me with her big brown eyes, her ears up as high as they can go, as if she wants to hear more about them. So I tell her about how my mom met Bennett's mom when we were babies and how Micayla came to Seagate the summer before second grade. She sits close to me, not making a peep, with her lips curved up slightly in what I like to call her listening smile.

"Micayla's getting her hair braided this morning and I'm super jealous." I show Marilyn Monroe my boring straight hair. "I wonder what color beads she's going to get."

Marilyn Monroe listens to me, but I can tell she's getting bored. She probably doesn't think much about human hair problems.

"You still want Daisy's," I say. "I can tell. We'll go later."

She jumps onto my lap and licks my face and then settles down.

"Oh, and this other thing happened since I saw you last," I tell her. "So there's this guy, you've probably seen him around, his name is Mr. Brookfield. Anyway, he can do this crazy scream, and it's been in movies."

I try to imitate the Scream, and it sounds really bad. And then Marilyn Monroe starts barking like crazy, like she's trying to imitate it too. And then I get worried we're going to wake Hudson up.

"Shh," I say, and she immediately gets what I'm saying and stops barking. "We make a good team, Marilyn Monroe."

Her lips go from her listening smile to her smiling smile, and I know she agrees.

7

It takes me a few days to come up with my best new idea, but I'm glad it didn't take all summer. I'm sitting on the bench outside Sundae Best eating espresso cookie ice cream in a sugar cone, and that's when I realize that you can feel so happy about something (espresso cookie ice cream) and so sad about something (Danish) at the exact same time. But you can also wipe away a sad thing with a happy thing. Temporarily, at least.

So I decide to make a pact with myself that whenever I start to get sad missing Danish, I immediately give myself something happy to think about. It's not hard to find happy things on Seagate, so my pact is pretty easy to keep.

Walking to Micayla's yesterday, I got sad because I saw a teenager walking an apricot poodle pretty much exactly Danish's size. My throat started to get a sunburny feeling, and I immediately wanted to turn around and go home. But then I passed a pretty white house with a million beach pails lined up on the ledge of the front porch.

I stopped for a second and wondered why I'd never noticed it before. Maybe because Micayla usually picks me up and we walk the other way to the beach? Or maybe because I've been looking down as I walk this summer since I'm feeling so sad?

But it didn't matter why I'd never seen it before—I was seeing it now. And it was the picture of happiness. You can never have too many beach pails, and these were all different colors—turquoise, hot pink, yellow, Kelly green. Some handles were up; some were down. It didn't look arranged in any artful way, but that made it even more beautiful.

So basically, whenever I get sad about Danish, I will think about those beach pails. I'll try to remember all the different colors and the order they were in, and then sometimes I'll stop just to visit them and see if they've changed.

It's such a simple thing, but seeing it made me so happy.

I even snapped a picture with my phone before anyone inside caught me doing it. If they did catch me, I figured I'd just tell them how much I loved it.

I pick Micayla up and show her the house, and then we walk together to meet Bennett. After we pick him up by the Ping-Pong stadium, the three of us are going to the free concert by the gazebo in the middle of the island. They have concerts every Wednesday, and we try to be the first ones there. It doesn't really matter if we like the band or not, we just like sitting right up front and then dancing like maniacs.

We started doing this the summer we were eight, and we've been doing it ever since. Only, back then, our moms would have to take us, and they'd tell us to calm down, asking us if we could just sit and relax and enjoy the music. We were enjoying it, though—just in our own way.

Micayla's been doing this thing lately: No matter where we're going, she takes me past Dog Beach. It started that she just wanted to take me there to help me stop feeling so sad about Danish. But now it seems like something else is going on.

Mason Redmond, who we've known forever, is helping out at Dog Beach this summer. He doesn't really do much except encourage people to pick up after the dogs and occasionally throw a ball around, but he says it's helpful for him because he wants to be a veterinarian one day. He's only eleven, like us, but my mom says he's a forward thinker. I guess she means that he plans ahead.

I'm pretty sure Micayla has a crush on Mason, but she hasn't admitted it yet. Micayla started having crushes last summer, when we were only going into fifth grade. I didn't have any crushes, but it was kind of fun to talk to Micayla about hers. Micayla's older sister, Ivy, always has crushes, so maybe that's why Micayla got them earlier than me.

The crushes only lasted like three days, anyway. I feel like when I get a crush, it will last a long time.

This summer, though, she's been acting all funny when she sees Mason. She doesn't want to get too close, but he has to be within sight. She wants to wait a few minutes, and then when she thinks that Mason sees us, she wants to leave.

I don't really get it.

Plus, we've known Mason as long as we've known each other—since the summer before second grade. That's when Micayla's family bought the house here, and that's when Mason started spending summers on Seagate with his aunt and uncle.

He's just an average kid, except for his whole "forward thinking" thing.

"Okay, let's go," Micayla says five minutes after we've gotten to Dog Beach. I timed it, because I was wondering if we were actually staying for such a short amount of time or if I was just imagining it. You know how they say time flies when you're having fun? I thought it could have been that kind of thing. But it isn't—it's just Micayla's secret crush.

"Already?" I ask. "I wanted to play with the pair of Malteses again."

"Sorry, Rem, we'll be late for the concert," Micayla tells me, grabbing my hand and gently pulling me away. At the same time, I notice Mason hopping off the lifeguard's chair and walking closer to us. "And you spent all morning hanging out with Marilyn Monroe, so you're not too dog-deprived."

Sooner or later Mason's going to start thinking that we really hate him, but I don't want to tell Micayla that. Since she hasn't yet told me about her crush, we haven't been mentioning Mason at all.

When we get to the concert, Bennett's in front, in our usual spot, and he's saving us seats. But as we get closer, I notice that he's with those twins again. They're everywhere.

They're sitting on the grass, texting or playing games on their phones, and they barely say hi to us. I want to ask Bennett why they're here, but I know that would be rude.

Finally the music starts. It's one of the local Seagate bands. I don't think the band members play together during the year, but once summer comes, they play all over the island—at the free concerts, at the coffee shops, at baby music classes in the mornings, even at some of the beach bonfires.

The band is called Saturday We Tennis, which doesn't really make any sense, and none of us know what it means. When you first hear it, you probably think it means that they play tennis on Saturdays, but Micayla guessed that Saturday is actually the name of a person they play tennis with. We don't even know if they play tennis.

Anyway, the band is three guys named Everett, Aiden, and George, and they're in college, but they all grew up spending summers on Seagate.

They're pretty much our local celebrities.

Their most popular song is called "Photo Booth Jam," and it's kind of silly, describing all the kinds of pictures people take in photo booths. Micayla, Bennett, and I know all the words, of course, so we stand up and start singing along with them. Aiden always encourages audience participation.

After a few minutes, Avery Sanders joins us in our section. She high-fives me when she sees me and then starts dancing with us.

"Silly face with glasses," I sing. "Oh yeah."

"Kissy face with Amy," Micayla sings. "Oh yeaaaahhh." The end of that verse drags on, and she does it perfectly.

"Thumbs-up! High five! Fish face, smooch, eyebrow twist." This is the part of the song that starts to go really fast, and Bennett can totally keep up with them. They usually find Bennett in the crowd after and tell him that he can fill in if one of them gets sick.

Bennett gets all excited when they tell him this, and I think he secretly hopes one of them does get sick so he can be in the band. So far it hasn't happened. But it would be so cool to see Bennett up there. I'd cheer for him as loud as I possibly could.

"That song was really crazy," Claire says, as we're applauding. "I mean, photo booths are fun and everything, but who sings about them?" She looks at us to agree with her, but obviously we're not going to.

"Shh," I say. "They could hear you. And their feelings would get hurt."

"What?" She makes a face at me. "They're grown-ups in a band. You don't need to worry about them, Remy."

She didn't say much, but the few words she did say made

me feel like the stupidest, most immature person in the world. I don't know how she was able to accomplish that so quickly.

And I don't know why she even came down here if all she was going to do was insult the songs of one of our favorite bands.

I remember how my mom always tells me to ignore the kids at school when they say dumb things, so I try to do that now. But it seems harder than usual, like I'm out of practice.

I never had to worry about stuff like this on Seagate before, and I shouldn't have to worry about it now. This Claire girl doesn't even belong here, especially because she doesn't want to be here in the first place.

The band starts playing their next song, "Friend Me," and this one is really fast-paced, and Micayla and I always hold hands and dance around to it while Bennett sings as loud as he can.

I'm about to hop up and start dancing when I notice that Micayla and Bennett are staying seated. It doesn't take me long to figure out why—they're embarrassed in front of Claire.

Don't they know that she doesn't really matter?

Ever since Claire and Calvin got to Seagate, I've noticed that I have been thinking really mean thoughts. I never thought these things about people before. Sure, I really don't like wheelie-backpack girls in my school, but I pretty much just stay away from them.

But with Calvin and Claire here, I'm turning into a mean person.

After a few weeks on Seagate, they started complaining to their mom that they were really bored, so she signed them up for two weeks of tennis camp in Westchester, near where they live. And when I found that out, I was ecstatically happy. Too happy. I felt bad about how happy I was. But they were just such a drag to have around. They were always complaining, and Bennett was always trying to include them in things, and then they would still complain.

So now they're gone and it's just Bennett, Micayla, and me again. I still miss Danish, but things are starting to feel close to right.

The annual Seagate Fourth of July Celebration is great, the way it always is: fireworks on the beach, the staff from Shazamburger grilling hot dogs and hamburgers on the boardwalk, enough for everyone on the island to have two of each.

There's a pickle-eating contest, but Bennett is grossed out by pickles, so we never stick around for that. There's a line at Sundae Best that wraps around the whole island, practically, but no one seems to mind. No one worries about their kids staying up late, because everyone can just sleep in the next day. That's the beauty of Seagate: No one is in a rush. Time doesn't really matter, because everyone has so much of it.

"Y'know that kid Mason Redmond?" Bennett asks us as we're on the way to the beach. I'm starting to get a sense that he knows about Micayla's crush, but I'm not sure. Bennett was never involved in our crush talk last summer, even though he was around us all the time. I'm not sure how that worked out, but it did.

We nod.

"He knows what he wants to do when he grows up," Bennett says. "Do you think that's weird or cool?"

"Weird," I jump right in. "Kids should be kids, I think."

Micayla laughs. "You always talk like a grown-up, though, Remy!"

"You know what I mean, Mic." I nudge her with my shoulder.

Bennett ignores our little back-and-forth. "But he's our age, so how does he know he wants to be a veterinarian? And why is he working on it over the summer?" He seems really concerned, but there's no reason to be.

"Don't worry," I tell Bennett. "We're kids. We can just focus on being kids. That's what my mom always tells me."

"My mom tells me that sixth grade at my school is going to be really serious and I'm going to need to buckle down," Bennett says. "I don't even know what that means, and isn't that a weird expression?"

"Yeah," Micayla says. "I don't think of buckles as being down; I think of them as, like, being through something."

They go back and forth about the expression, and then I start laughing, because the whole thing just sounds so silly.

I say, "Guys, we really only get two months of summer, so let's just enjoy it and not think about school, okay?"

They nod.

I'm not sure they agree with me, but at least they go along for the moment. We never used to talk about what we want to do when we grow up. Talking about it now gives me a funny feeling, like I'm lost in a crowd and can't find Bennett or Micayla anywhere.

We're almost at the beach when a poster catches my eye. It's haphazardly stuck to one of the streetlights with masking tape, and it has a picture of a dog on it.

"Guys, hang on one second," I say. "I have to look at this."

Micayla and Bennett hang back, and I hear them talking about the whole "knowing what you want to do when you grow up" thing, and I try to tune it out. I'm not sure when my friends became so serious, but I think I liked them better before.

The poster says:

OUR BELOVED OSCAR IS MISSING!

Help us find our amazing boxer Oscar. He has brown fur everywhere except his stomach and his paws, where he has white fur. He answers to the names Oscar, Oscie, or Cuddle Cookies (don't ask). Email DawnRam200@gmail.com if you find him.
Reward if found and returned.
Thank you!

I stand there for a second after reading the sign. Then I rip it down. For the first time in forever, I have this feeling like I really need to do something. I have to find Oscar. I know how hard it is to be without a pet, but these people don't have to. And especially since I've become so attached to Marilyn Monroe, the sting of missing a pet feels even more brutal.

"You guys." I run over to them. "We have to find this dog." I show them the poster, then feel a little bit guilty for ripping it down. Other people need to see it too, if we're going to be able to find Oscar. But I also need to take it with us—I need to keep looking at his picture to remember what Oscar looks like, and I need to keep the email address handy for when we find him.

"I've definitely seen this dog around," Micayla says. "Should we go ask Mason at Dog Beach?"

I cover my mouth and try not to laugh. This crush is becoming totally obvious.

"No, let's not talk to Mason," Bennett says. "He stresses me out. I thought summer reading was enough to be worried about, but now I have to think about my career?" Bennett shakes his head. "I can't handle that kid this summer."

I walk them over to one of the wooden benches on the path to the beach, and we sit down for a second to talk. "Plus, don't you think Dog Beach would be the first place that his owners would look for Oscar?" I ask.

"You're probably right," Micayla says, slightly defeated.

"Do you know Oscar's family?" I ask them. "I think he looks familiar, but I'm not sure. Danish usually stayed away from the bigger dogs."

"Danish was a little wimpy," Bennett says, and then moves back a little bit because he knows I'm about to hit him.

I hit his arm anyway. "Hey! Bennett Newhouse, take that back!"

"Come on, Rem, we loved him, but he tried to drink coffee out of your dad's mug that one time. He didn't even like doggie treats; he always wanted his own croissant from Mornings."

Bennett's right about that. We said it again and again that Danish was more human than canine, and he did sometimes prefer a croissant from Mornings to a treat from Daisy's. The owners of Mornings (Seagate's fanciest breakfast place) are a couple named Beverly and Sidney, and they're really *not* dog people. I guess Danish knew that, and he was constantly trying to get them to change their mind.

Danish was never allowed inside, but I'd usually get him his own croissant. They made him so happy. How could I refuse him?

We all agree that we've seen Oscar around but we're not sure where, and we're not sure who he was with. So we take the poster and we walk around Seagate and go up to as many people as we can, asking, "Have you seen this dog?"

Most people shake their heads.

One old lady says, "I think I saw him at Daisy's. He was stealing treats from the other dogs! No one did anything to stop him!" She shakes her head like it was a complete travesty, and then she walks away.

Micayla suggests that we ask Avery Sanders. "She's such a gossip, and she knows everybody, so she'd probably be able to help."

She has a point, and I haven't seen Avery in a few days, come to think of it. The last time I saw her was at the Wednesday concert when Claire made us feel bad about dancing.

After a few more minutes of searching, I can tell that Micayla and Bennett really want to go to the beach. It's not hard to figure it out, since Micayla keeps saying, "Can we take a break, Rem? I really want to swim. They said it might rain later."

And Bennett says, "Let's go looking again tonight. Everyone's out now, and Oscar's probably scared and hiding."

I don't know if boxers even get scared. I think they're often used as watchdogs and sometimes help the police catch criminals. I was reading a book on dog breeds at the school library so I could help my parents choose our next dog, and I seem to remember that.

"You guys can go," I tell them. "I'm going to keep looking."

They tell me to stop being crazy and that of course they're coming, but a few minutes later they go to the beach for real, and I'm left walking around alone.

I don't know why it's so important to me that I find Oscar, but it really is. I guess it's because my dog-free life is pretty permanent right now, but Oscar's family's life doesn't have to be.

After a few hours of looking, I still haven't been able to find Oscar the boxer, and I have to go home. I even stopped to ask Amber and to quickly say hi to Marilyn Monroe, but neither of them had any information.

On the way home, I see Avery sitting on the bench outside Novel Ideas, Seagate's bookstore.

"Hi, Remy," she says. "You look lost, but I know that's impossible."

"Oh." I laugh. "Yeah, I'd never be lost on Seagate. But maybe you can help me?" I tell her the whole story about Oscar the boxer, but unfortunately she doesn't have any clues.

"Where's Micayla?" she asks, folding down the corner of a page of the novel she's reading.

I shrug. "Home, I guess?"

"Oh, okay. I'll call her later."

It seems weird that Avery's calling Micayla, since we're pretty much "see you around" friends, but I guess things can change.

The whole way home, I keep my eyes peeled for Oscar the boxer. I know his name is just Oscar, but I think *Oscar the boxer* sounds so cute. I'm starting to get worried that he jumped into the ocean and swam away when no one was looking. Dogs are good swimmers, and he could probably make it to the mainland somewhere, but I'm not sure how anyone would ever find him then.

"You really think he has tags and identification?" I ask my dad while he's making dinner. It's stir-fried-chicken night. Aside from his famous salmon casserole, it's the only thing my dad makes, but his stir-fry is actually edible.

"I do, Remy." He turns around from the stove and smiles at me. "Can you grab some plates? Do you want to eat inside or out?"

"Out," I tell him. I grab our wooden tray with the blue-and-white tile, the one I use when I serve my parents breakfast in bed. I only do that once a year, on their anniversary, which is August 14, so we leave the tray on Seagate. I stack the tray with plates and silverware, fill up two tall glasses with pink lemonade, and bring everything out to the back porch.

My dad brings out the sizzling frying pan and the bowl from the rice cooker and puts everything out on the picnic table. When my mom serves dinner, she puts everything onto serving platters and into fancy bowls, but my dad serves the food in whatever he cooked it in. To me, that just makes sense. Fewer dishes to wash.

"Do you think Mom's going to get in trouble?" Dad asks, putting some stir-fry on my plate.

"She didn't read the book again?"

"Nope!"

My mom loves reading, but she hates the books that her book club picks. They're usually dark and depressing, about a war or a missing child or a woman leaving her husband. I don't read them—my mom just tells me about them, usually explaining why she wasn't able to get through the book.

She keeps going to the book club meetings anyway, because she loves seeing her friends there—Bennett's mom, Micayla's mom, her other friends Barbara, Faye, and Gina. To be honest, they may never actually discuss books; they might spend the whole time talking about their families and stuff. I don't really know.

But when Mom goes out, it's just Dad and me for dinner, and sometimes that's really nice too. I used to wish I had a sibling, but I've gotten pretty used to being an only child. Maybe I'm kind of like Danish that way—I enjoy spending time with adults, even a little bit more than I like spending time with kids, the same way he preferred people to dogs.

I ask my dad a million more questions about where he thinks Oscar might be, and then he tells me that maybe we can go out searching for him after dinner, after the dishes are done. We can search for Oscar and meet Mom at the book club and maybe get ice cream for the walk home.

But as we're doing the dishes, which really only involves loading the dishwasher and hoping Mom doesn't notice that we didn't rinse everything first, we hear a knock on the door.

I immediately assume it's Mom coming home early. Which is disappointing because it means we probably won't go out for ice cream. But when I get to the door, I see that it's Bennett. And he's holding a leash.

My heart starts pounding. Did Bennett buy me a dog? I immediately get excited and scared all at once. Maybe my parents will be upset at first but then they'll say we can keep him, of course. Or maybe it's a girl dog. I don't know. I'll pretend that I'm mad at Bennett for doing that, but of course I'll be thrilled.

But then I get some sense. Bennett didn't buy me a dog. Where would he find one, first of all? And he'd never go behind my parents' back for something like that—or anything, really.

I look closer. Attached to the leash that Bennett is holding is Oscar!

"You found him?" I scream, and then I hear a dish break, and my dad comes running in. Oops. It's a good thing we don't use Mom's fancy platters.

"What's going on?" my dad asks.

"I don't know!" I yell. I'm so pumped up that I can't stop shouting.

"I was walking back from the pool after Asher's swimming lesson, and I saw a dog wandering around outside that store that sells all the beachy decorations."

"Beach House is the name of the store. Yeah?" I don't know why we're stopping this story for such insignificant details, even though I really do love that store.

"Maybe he was hungry and wandered over from Shazamburger? I don't know," Bennett says. "But I looked closer. I told Asher to sit down on the bench because I wanted to see if it was really Oscar, but I was nervous that maybe it wasn't and maybe the dog would bite Asher. Y'know?"

"Yeah!" I yell again. Sometimes it takes Bennett forever to tell a story.

"So I looked closer! And it was Oscar. He had tags and everything!" Bennett is yelling now too, and my dad backs away a little bit. "His fur is all wet. Maybe he was swimming in the ocean, like you said?"

"Yeah!"

I realize I am saying the same thing over and over again, but I can't stop because I am totally freaking out. Bennett found Oscar! Sure, I wish I was the one to find him, but at least he's been found. Then it occurs to me—if he's found, why did Bennett bring him here?

"Wait. Bennett." I pause to catch my breath, and my dad goes back into the kitchen, probably to pick up the broken pieces from the plate he dropped a few minutes ago. "Did you contact the owners?"

He sits down on the little bench outside our front door, the one Grandma always used to take off her muddy shoes after gardening. "I was about to," he says. "But then I had to come here first. You were really the one searching for him, and I just happened to see him. So I think you should contact the owners. You should get the reward and the credit."

"Bennett," I say, and all of a sudden I want to sit down next to him and give him a kiss on the cheek, even though I haven't done that for at least five years. "You found him. And they're probably worried sick. So we should tell them soon—or tell them right now, actually!"

"Let's go," he says. "But first, do you have any of those treats that Danish used to love?"

I'm sure we have them. I saw them at the back of the pantry a few days ago, and I wanted to tell my parents to throw them out, but I couldn't get up the courage to say anything.

At first it feels weird to give Oscar one of Danish's treats, but then it feels like the absolute right thing to do.

I go back inside and grab the box and then tell Dad we're going to bring Oscar back to his owners. His address, 87 Sand Lane (two streets away from me), is written right there on the little dog-bone charm hanging from his collar.

We give Oscar a few treats and take the box with us. His owners will probably be happy to have them. It's not always easy to find good dog treats on Seagate, and we always got Danish the best.

For a dog who has been missing from his family, Oscar

doesn't seem that upset. He's happy with his treats, and he's playing with me like he's known me his whole life.

Either I'm really good with dogs (and I know that I am, but I don't like to brag about it) or Oscar is really good with people.

It could be both, actually.

10

We almost ring the doorbell at Oscar's owners' house before we realize that someone's already sitting out on the front porch. Then I hear a small cry, and I turn and see a tired woman pushing a stroller with three seats in it.

"Triplets," she whispers. I wonder why she's not screaming with joy that we have Oscar with us, but it's because she hasn't seen him yet. He's hiding behind me—until he hears the woman's voice. When he sees her, he jumps up on her, and then jumps up a little bit more so that he can see inside the stroller. He starts panting and wagging his tail furiously and licking the lady's face. And she's so excited to see him, but I think she's trying to stay quiet too, since the babies are sleeping.

Bennett starts telling the story of how he found Oscar but stops himself when he notices the stroller.

Then all three of us are just standing there in silence, but our smiles are speaking louder than our voices ever could. It's like that whole "a picture is worth a thousand words" thing, except it's not a picture, it's the real thing.

The lady puts a finger to her lips in the universal *shh* sign and motions for us to follow her inside. She leaves the jumbo stroller out on the porch. If that's not a sign that Seagate is the safest place in the whole world, I don't know what is.

Oscar runs inside like it's the happiest day of his life, and we follow behind. Inside on the couch we find a sleeping man. I'm guessing he's the father of the babies. The TV is still on, and he's holding the remote as if he's about to change the channel, but he's totally asleep.

It's the kind of funny picture you'd see posted online for everyone to email to their friends, only I don't think I should be the one to take it.

The lady exhales and fills Oscar's water bowl, and he runs over.

"We gave him water," I say. "Don't worry."

"I'm not worried." She grins at us. "I'm just so grateful that you found him. Please sit down. Can I get you a drink? Please tell me how you found him."

Bennett starts the story again. "I was waiting for my brother at his swim lesson, and then I saw Oscar roaming around. I recognized him from the picture and also because there aren't many dogs on Seagate with brown fur every-where except their stomachs and their paws." Oscar walks over to us, and Bennett starts petting him. Then Oscar sits on the floor between us and we're both petting him. He has soft fur—wiry and silky—and it seems to fall out all over the place. His owner must spend all day vacuuming.

"So I checked his collar," Bennett continues, "and it was definitely him. I had to stop at Remy's first, though, because Remy was the one who really started everyone on this mission to find your dog."

The lady raises her eyebrows. "You're Remy?" she asks.

I nod.

"Wow. You are one special girl," the lady says. "And let me just say that Oscar doesn't respond this way to just everyone. He seems to really like you guys."

"Thanks. He's an awesome dog." I smile. "This is Bennett. Did we already say that?"

I crack up and realize that I'm feeling kind of nervous all of a sudden, though I don't know why.

"I'm Dawn Ramirez," she says. "The exhausted, sleeping man on the couch is my husband, Mateo. And Oscar is my first baby. I don't even know how he got out. Maybe he's feeling neglected. We have triplets—you probably noticed." She laughs and then takes a deep breath. "And it's pretty crazy. All I can say is, thank you guys so, so much for finding him."

"You're welcome," I say. "It was all Bennett."

"It was pretty much all Remy," he says, hitting me gently on the arm. "If you didn't mention it, I wouldn't have paid attention."

"Well, I'm giving you both the reward," she says. She leaves the room for a minute and then comes back with two envelopes. One for Bennett and one for me.

She sits down at the table and asks us if we want ice cream. While she's dishing it out into bowls from the to-go containers from Sundae Best, we hear screaming. Really loud baby screaming. It's coming in surprisingly clear, since they're out on the front porch.

Then Bennett points to a flashing gray walkie-talkie-like device. I'm guessing it's some kind of baby monitor, and I understand why Dawn was so comfortable leaving the triplets sleeping outside.

"They sleep best out there," she explains. "I'm going to give it a second and see if she falls asleep."

"You can tell which one is crying just by listening?" I ask.

She nods. "That was Mia. The other two are boys, Felipe and Alexander. Mia's cry is distinct, and she cries the most." Dawn puts her head down on the table and stares at the monitor. Bennett and I eat our ice cream quietly and quickly. I think we're both getting the feeling that it's almost time to go.

"Listen, I'm going to ask you something," Dawn says. "You can totally say no. I'm sure you're busy and everything. But Oscar really responded well to you. And as you can probably tell, I'm in over my head with these babies. Would you be interested in watching him? Like a dog sitter? Walks, trips to Dog Beach, stuff like that? We'd pay you and everything, of course."

Bennett and I look at each other. I think he's talking with his eyes, the way we used to do when we were little, but I can't be sure. The summer we were seven, Bennett and I made up this intricate blinking code, so that we would always be able to communicate, even when other people were around. Micayla tried to learn it too, but it was really just a thing between Bennett and me.

I can't wait any longer to figure out if Bennett wants to do this or not. If Calvin and Claire were here, he might say no. But they're away, and so Bennett's my friend again, the way he used to be.

"I'd love to," I say. "Dogs are my favorite animal, and we spend a lot of time at Dog Beach, anyway."

"Oh, you have a dog?" Dawn asks.

Now Bennett is blinking a little too much, and I know he's speaking with his eyes; that was our code for danger, which ultimately became our code for when people asked us awkward questions, like if we were going to get married someday, or when we'd eat dinner over at Mrs. Shanley's house and she'd try to serve us mushy cauliflower.

"I used to," I tell Dawn. "He died this past year."

She nods. "Are you guys brother and sister?"

Bennett and I widen our eyes—the signal for shock, which is probably not a very good secret code, but we never came up with anything better.

"No," Bennett says, laughing a little. "We're just friends."

Brother and sister? We look nothing alike. Bennett has

floppy brown hair that usually falls into his eyes until his mom bribes him to get a haircut. My hair is somewhere between blonde and brown. Plus, Bennett's, like, three inches taller than I am.

I don't know why that question bothers me.

I hate it when people ask us if we're in love or if we're going to get married. We're only eleven and it's a dumb question. But now I'm annoyed that Dawn asked us if we're brother and sister.

Something in the way Bennett says "We're just friends" makes me upset. It's true. We are just friends. But not like any pair of friends you'd find in a school or on a soccer team or something. We're different. We're lifelong Seagate friends. Best friends, even.

All our lives Bennett told everyone that I was his best friend. I have two best friends—Bennett and Micayla—but as far as I knew, I was Bennett's only best friend. And I liked it that way.

I wonder why he didn't say it just now.

I wonder if things changed and I didn't even notice.

"I'm sorry about your dog," Dawn says, and I remember that's what we were talking about before I got distracted about me and Bennett. "It's really hard to lose a dog. I've been through it a few times, and it never gets easier."

"Yeah, that's what people say," I mumble. I want to finalize the arrangements for watching Oscar and then I want to go home. It suddenly feels awkward being in this kitchen, and even though there's still a spoonful of ice cream left, I don't really feel like eating it.

"Well, why don't you take a day to think it over? And if you're interested in dog-sitting for Oscar, come by tomorrow. I usually take the babies out for a morning walk, but we're never too far." She smiles. "That's the beauty of Seagate, right?"

"Yup!" I stand up and put my bowl in the sink, and Bennett follows me. "I'm a mother's helper right now for Amber Seasons on Monday and Wednesday mornings, but I'm free the other days."

"Okay. Well, we'd work around your schedule, of course. Thank you guys so much again," Dawn says as she's walking us to the door. "If I wasn't so tired, I'd sound more excited, but please know how absolutely, completely grateful I am."

We leave Dawn's house, and the triplets are now sleeping peacefully in their gigantic stroller. I wonder how long they sleep outside, or if they ever move into their cribs. They can't possibly sleep out here all night; it gets chilly.

Bennett's house is closer to Dawn's than to mine, but he walks me home anyway. He says his dad always tells him that it's safer for boys to walk alone than it is for girls. On Seagate, though, it's safe for anyone to walk alone. But I don't argue, because I like his company. Even right now, when we're not really talking, it's just nice to walk together. And the nicest thing about being best friends is that you can walk in complete silence and not feel weird about it.

Sometimes you just don't have anything to say, and that's okay.

It's quiet for so long that I'm startled when Bennett asks, "Wasn't it weird that she thought we were brother and sister?"

I'm surprised he's thinking about it too, but in a way I'm glad I'm not the only one who still is.

"Yeah," I say. "Are they new here? I don't think I've seen them before. Or maybe I just don't recognize her now that she has the babies."

"Huh?"

"I mean, maybe Dawn and her husband were the kind of couple who were always going out to eat late at night and staying in their cabana by the beach and weren't really out and about. And they're completely different people now with the triplets."

"Oh. Yeah. That could be."

After I say it, I realize that every change in life—big or small—can change you as a person. The way having babies changed Dawn and Amber. I wonder how I've changed since Danish died. I know I've changed, but I wonder how exactly, and if everyone can tell.

All this change can be frustrating if things are good and all you want is for them to stay the same. That's part of the beauty of hanging out with dogs: They're pretty predictable. They like to eat and go out for walks and have belly rubs. And they'll always be there to greet you and welcome you home.

When we get to my house, Bennett tells me he'll see me in the morning. He'll come by and then we'll walk to Micayla's, and we'll all bring Asher over to day camp. We used to go to Seagate day camp, and it was fun, but now we're old enough to entertain ourselves. And that's even better.

At home, it's probably annoying for Bennett to help out with Asher so much. But here he doesn't seem to mind it. Everyone wants to be walking around on Seagate anyway, because there are so many people out and about, and you don't have to worry about cars, and no one is in a hurry. Plus, Bennett doesn't have to take Asher everywhere by himself; he has Micayla and me to go with him.

It doesn't really matter what we do together—we always have fun.

One time we spent a whole afternoon throwing pebbles across the walkway to the beach. It was a rainy day, so no one was really walking there, and we made up this whole game, seeing how far the pebbles could go. Most people would have probably thought it was really dumb, but we loved it.

That's just the kind of friends we are.

I don't really need a day to think about Dawn's job offer. Of course I am going to watch Oscar. We bonded immediately. I have Marilyn Monroe, and she's great, but it's kind of like the saying that you can never have too many friends. You can never have too many dog friends either!

Plus, I feel a little bit bad for Oscar. He was Dawn's first baby (she even said it herself), and now she doesn't really have time for him. I wonder how often dogs are replaced by babies. It makes sense, I guess, but it must be really hard for the dog.

There should be some kind of doggie support group where they could go and bark as loud and as often as they need to and get out their frustrations. Maybe Oscar ran away because he needed attention and wasn't getting it.

Poor guy. I want to help him.

My Oscar-watching time might cut into my Micayla and Bennett time, but I'm sure we can work it out. We've navigated the two mornings I'm with Marilyn Monroe, and we can navigate this too.

I daydream a perfect schedule while I eat my Froot Loops on the front porch and wait for Bennett and Micayla to get here.

My parents are at the Seagate Art Festival today. It starts at ten, but they got special passes for the early exhibit that started at eight. I don't think anything is worth getting up at eight in the morning, but they do. I'm just glad they didn't make me go with them.

They are making me meet them there later, to see the special exhibit on Minnie Lions, an artist who spent her whole life on Seagate, photographing everyday objects. My parents are obsessed with her work, and I'm a fan too.

I'm excited to see it, just not so early in the morning.

In my perfect schedule, I would watch Oscar in the mornings, bring him back to his home, and then maybe watch him again in the afternoons. That way I can spend the middle chunk of the day with my friends. That's when we go swimming or surfing or just relax on the beach.

I finish my Froot Loops and then run upstairs to put on a bathing suit. It's so easy to get dressed on Seagate. Breakfast in pajamas, never worrying about what to wear for the day—always just a bathing suit with shorts and a T-shirt over it. When I was little, I would walk around Seagate in only a bathing suit and no one minded, but now it just feels awkward to do that.

When you think about bathing suits too much, you realize how weird they are. You're pretty much just wearing underwear, but underwear that everyone can see.

I'm upstairs changing into my turquoise-and-white two-piece when I hear Bennett and Micayla downstairs. I quickly make sure my door is closed. The safety of Seagate is also a little bit nerve-racking—friends can walk into your house anytime, including when you're changing!

When I'm dressed, I find them downstairs looking through one of my mom's furniture catalogs and eating Cheerios out of the box.

"This chair is way awesome," Bennett says. "It's like a chair bed. Right? Doesn't it look big enough to sleep on?"

"Sure." Micayla turns the page.

I wonder how long I can stand here without them noticing me. It's strange how engrossed they are in this catalog. My mom is obsessed with furniture, so she subscribes to tons of magazines, and pretty much every furniture designer in the world sends her a catalog. The same way I like to imagine perfect schedules, she likes to daydream about redecorating.

If it were up to her, she'd redecorate every year. She loves changing things up. And I'm exactly the opposite. If it were up to me, my room on Seagate would still look the way it did when Grandma owned the house. And my room in Manhattan would look the same way it did when I was a little girl.

I just like things to stay the same.

"Oh, hey, Rem," Bennett says. Is it possible that he's gotten taller in just one day? Looking at him sitting in one of our wooden kitchen chairs, it seems like his head is a whole foot above Micayla's. I wonder if it was always like this and I just didn't notice. "People are setting up the Sandcastle Contest and I said I'd help. Micayla's in too. You're gonna come, right?"

We always help set up the Sandcastle Contest. We help get all the supplies organized and hang the banners and walk around Seagate getting people to sign up. But I'd totally forgotten about it. I need to go to Dawn's and tell her that I will help with Oscar.

Then I realize that Bennett and I never officially said we were going to watch Oscar together, but Dawn asked him too—not just me. In my head, I made the decision that I'd do it, but I don't know if he did. And he's actually the one who found Oscar in the first place.

I reach into the box for a handful of Cheerios. I never get sick of cereal. I could eat cereal all day, every day, and be fine with it.

"Oh, what'd you decide to do about watching Oscar?" Bennett asks as if he read my mind. "I really want to, but it's going to be hard on the days I have to walk Asher to and from camp. My mom ended up taking him today because I forgot about the Sandcastle Contest."

"I want to do it," I tell them with my mouth full of Cheerios. It sounds gross, but sometimes it's okay to be gross with your best friends.

"What are you guys talking about?" Micayla asks. "Anything I should know about?"

Micayla was out to dinner at Picnic last night for her parents' anniversary. Picnic is Seagate's fanciest restaurant, and it's a really ironic name. When people think about picnics, they think casual and sitting on the grass and stuff, but this place is super fancy—white tablecloths, tall crystal glasses just for water, and even the salads cost a lot of money. The food is good, but it's the kind of place where you have to whisper during the meal, and eating there always takes forever. It's not really my kind of restaurant.

So we tell Micayla the whole story, and she says, "Well, I want to watch Oscar too!"

I look at Bennett and he looks at me and again I wonder if we're talking with our eyes or not. We're going to have to have a real conversation with words about whether we can still talk with our eyes.

"Remember how I was the one who was really able to communicate with Danish?" Micayla reminds us. "I mean, I have a gift. I'm practically Mary Poppins."

We were obsessed with that movie when we were little, especially the parts when Mary was able to communicate with Andrew, the dog. So over the years, Micayla convinced us that she was able to have conversations with dogs too.

Danish would bark, and Micayla would talk, and then

Danish would bark back. But his pitch would always change, and it really seemed like Micayla understood what his barks meant, and that Danish understood Micayla's words.

I had totally forgotten about that, even though I have conversations with Marilyn Monroe all the time. But I didn't think I had magical powers—the conversations just seemed normal to me.

"I don't think Dawn would mind," Bennett says. "And it would really help to have more people, especially when I have to watch Asher and you guys have to do, um, more lying on the beach."

We both hit Bennett at the same time, and he says, "Ouch. I'm getting beaten up by girls!"

We all agree that we'd love to watch Oscar, so we decide to head over to Dawn's right away so that we can get to the Sandcastle Contest prep on time.

Dawn answers the door with one baby in one of those carrier things, one baby over her shoulder, and the third one crying in a swing behind her. Oscar is running around in circles barking and pushing his metal bowl with his nose.

"Oh, I am so glad to see you guys!" I'm not even sure if she notices that Micayla, who she's never met, is with us. "Oscar is hungry and needs to go out. The food is in the cabinet next to the stove. Thanks, guys!"

She leaves us standing in the foyer, puts one baby down on a pillow on the couch, and picks up the crying one in the swing. It feels like she's immediately forgotten we're there. I guess that means we're just supposed to get started.

Bennett grabs the food. I pour some water into Oscar's other bowl. Micayla talks to him and pets him, and he calms down within seconds.

We really are a good team.

I go back to the living room to tell Dawn that we're leaving, but we find her on the couch, asleep, with three sleeping babies around her. Waking any of them up would probably be the worst thing we could do, so we tiptoe out with Oscar on his leash.

We walk him over to Dog Beach, which is luckily right near where the Sandcastle Contest prep is going on.

As soon as we get there, he runs onto the beach as if he's been waiting his whole life to get there. He starts playing with a French bulldog that we always see around. I think her name is Latte. Micayla walks off to start up a Mary Poppins–like conversation with that pair of Malteses we met the other day, and I keep an eye on Oscar, just to make sure he's playing nicely with others.

Bennett tells us he's going to check in with the Sandcastle Contest people.

I watch as he walks away, thinking back to that whole exchange with Dawn last night, the brother and sister thing, and the "We're just friends" thing. I don't know why I'm still thinking about it. It just seems to be stuck in my head, the way a burrito sits in your stomach hours after you eat it.

Bennett is Bennett. No one really spends much time

thinking about him. That sounds kind of mean, but it's just that I know him too well to have to wonder what's going on with him all the time.

Oscar goes over to get a drink of water out of this special doggie water fountain that Daisy Dog Lover Extraordinaire (that's what Daisy McDougal calls herself) had installed a few summers ago. I follow behind him and rub his belly for a minute. And then when I look up, I see Bennett walking toward me, but he's not alone.

He's with two other people.

The C Twins are back.

Bennett and Calvin take off to meet the Sandcastle Contest organizers, leaving me alone with Claire.

"I got kicked out of tennis camp," Claire tells me, digging her toes into the sand.

"Why? How?"

"If you let me talk, I'll tell you," she snaps.

I stay quiet.

"I got kicked out because I didn't want to play," she says, groaning. "I mean, seriously. My parents were paying for me to be there, so why did the counselors care if I played or not?"

I try not to look too confused. "Um? I guess because if you're not playing tennis, what are you really doing there?"

"Yeah, Remy. Thanks." Claire huffs and walks away, leaving me standing alone with Oscar. He seems tired and ready to go home, but I want to wait for Micayla and Bennett to get back before I head out.

Oscar goes back to playing and I sit down on a bench for a few minutes, feeling unsettled. I realize how good it felt when Calvin and Claire weren't here, but now they're back and Claire is being rude and surly and Bennett is busy with Calvin. I'm not sure where Micayla is, but I get this lonely feeling where I just want to go home and crawl under my covers.

I wish Danish were here. Oscar's nice and all, but he's not my dog.

So far, day one of the three of us watching Oscar is turning into me watching him. By myself.

"Remy, right?" I look up and see Mr. Brookfield, Claire and Calvin's grandpa, standing over me.

I nod.

"You running a doggie day care or something?" he asks. For a second I'm confused, and then I look down at my feet and see Oscar and two other dogs just sitting around me. I'm not even sure how or when the other two dogs got there.

"No, just watching one dog." I smile. But then I think about my time with Marilyn Monroe, and I wonder if Mr. Brookfield is on to something. Maybe I *am* on my path to running a doggie day care. "You guys don't have a dog, right?"

I don't ever remember seeing a dog running around inside or outside Mr. Brookfield's house, so I'm not sure what he's doing at Dog Beach.

"No, I just like coming to sit here," he says. "I like the benches. If you get up and stand on that one over there"—he points to the green bench a few feet away from us—"you can see the whole island. Try it sometime."

I want to try it right now, but I'm nervous that someone will see me doing it and tell Dawn that I'm not acting like a professional dog watcher.

"So you come here, just to sit, even though you don't have a dog?" I ask Mr. Brookfield.

"I do," he says. "The main section of beach doesn't have benches. And I don't want to carry a chair. Plus, I like to watch the pooches."

"There are chairs on the south end," I tell him. "When the Seagate Inn remodeled, they donated all their old lounges so that anyone who wanted a lounge chair could have one."

He nods. "That's true. But I'm good here."

I thought I was the only one who liked going to Dog Beach even without a dog.

I want to ask him something, but I don't know if I should. In all the years I have known Mr. Brookfield, I've never really talked to him before. I wonder if he was at Dog Beach all the times I was here with Danish and I never even noticed.

It's strange how you can see something all the time and not even realize it's there. It's like how when Mom rearranges the furniture and I promise myself that I'll remember how it used to look. But then after only a few days, I forget. Even though I saw it the old way for so long, I still can't remember.

In the distance, I see Bennett with a stack of posters that he'll have to hang up, reminding everyone about the Sandcastle Contest, and then I see Micayla talking to someone. It takes me a few seconds to figure out who it is, but when I squint my eyes, it's clear that it's Mason Redmond.

She's actually talking to her crush!

I'm excited and sad at the same time. They've probably forgotten about Oscar.

"So tell me more about that whole scream thing," I say finally, trying to think of something other than myself.

"I'm so glad you asked. What exactly would you like to know?" Mr. Brookfield asks. He stretches his legs out in front of him, and I notice he's wearing bright white sneakers and tall tube socks. It occurs to me that older people don't like to wear sandals as much as young people do. I wonder if there will come a time when I won't want to wear flip-flops every day. It's too sad to think about.

"How come nobody knows it's your scream that's in all those movies?" If Claire were here, she'd probably tell me to be quiet and that nobody really cares about it. But I do care. It's so mysterious.

I'm suddenly grateful that it's just Oscar, Mr. Brookfield, and me right now.

"I had a very small role in a movie, and I was grateful to get it," Mr. Brookfield tells me. "I'd been on a million auditions. In this one, I was cast as the person who was going to get attacked by an alligator. We shot the scene, and then the director told me they'd want to get the screaming sound just right, so we'd record it later. We did record it later, but the scene got cut considerably, so you could really only see the back of my head. And then eventually, even my head got cut. But the scream. Oh, that scream! They kept it. And for years and years, and still today, people are using that scream!"

Mr. Brookfield goes on, telling me details about some of the movies it's in, and it's clear he really does love to talk about this. I wish I'd known before, because I like hearing these kinds of stories. It took Claire to bring all this out of him.

The more Mr. Brookfield talks, the more I realize that he seems so much happier when he's talking about his work and when he's talking about the past and his wife and life on Seagate. He never seems that happy otherwise, just talking about day-to-day life.

"Remy!" Bennett runs over to me, all out of breath, and Calvin follows behind him. "They asked us to put up all these signs for the Sandcastle Contest right away. Are you okay bringing Oscar back by yourself?"

It's nice that he asked, but I wish he'd just come with me.

"Dude, she's fine," Calvin says. "It's Seagate."

Bennett looks at me again, and when I don't say anything right away, he says, "Yeah, you're right. We'll be around, Rem. See you soon."

They walk away with the signs flapping in their hands. Oscar is resting on the sand, and I think I've probably kept him out too long.

"Nice boy, that Bennett," Mr. Brookfield says. "He was always a nice boy."

"Yeah," I grumble. "I guess."

I take Oscar back home, where Dawn seems to be in better shape. Only one of the triplets is up, but he's not crying. The other two are sleeping in their swings.

"He looks exhausted! That's great!" Dawn gives me a hug. "Remy, I really want to thank you so much for taking care of Oscar."

"You're welcome." I laugh a little bit because I don't know what else to do. "Same time tomorrow morning?"

"Unless I need you before." She looks back at Oscar. "I'll text you?"

"Yeah, that would be great. See you later."

I walk back over to the beach, hoping that Calvin and Claire got bored with helping and decided to go back to Mr. Brookfield's to watch TV.

"Where did you go?" Micayla asks as soon as she sees me. She's sitting at the Sandcastle Contest registration table. "I texted you, like, seven times."

Uh-oh. I never even looked at my phone. I was so pre-occupied with thinking about Bennett and talking to Mr. Brookfield, I kind of forgot about Micayla. It's such a terrible thing to do, I feel guilty immediately.

"I didn't look at my phone. I don't know why. I'm so sorry!" I squish up my face in embarrassment and give Micayla a hug. "I had to take Oscar home. He was really tired."

"Yeah, I figured." She gives me a look that says *I'm confused* and *You're crazy* at the same time.

"Let's go help set up," I tell her. "I love looking at all the little tools some people use to build sandcastles."

"Me too," she says. "But I have to talk to you."

As we're walking over to get the supplies, I'm dying for Micayla to start talking, but we keep getting interrupted.

"Girls, all the supplies are on one of the picnic tables," Mrs. Pursuit tells us. "So far we have ten teams competing, so I'll need you to organize everything into ten bags and make sure every bag has one of each item."

"On it," I reply.

Mrs. Pursuit was a gym teacher in Connecticut before she retired. Now she lives on Seagate year-round, and the Sandcastle Contest was her idea. She gets really crazy when the day of the contest rolls around every summer. I'm pretty sure she thinks of it as the Olympics of sandcastle building.

Micayla, Bennett, and I were always a team, until last summer. The volunteers who usually help set up canceled at the last minute, and so Mrs. Pursuit asked us to step in.

We were so flattered, we didn't even mind stepping out of the contest.

We finally make it over to the picnic table and begin putting supplies into the royal blue tote bags, donated by Blueberry Crumble, Seagate's bakery.

I'm putting a sand sifter and a shovel into my fifth bag when I can't take the suspense anymore. "What did you have to talk to me about?" I ask.

"Oh, um, it was nothing," Micayla says.

"How could it be nothing?" I give her a crooked look. "Nothing is ever nothing, y'know. Between best friends, I mean."

I continue putting supplies into the bag and wait for her to talk.

She opens her mouth again but hesitates. "Well, I talked to Mason Redmond," she says.

It seems like there was something else she wanted to say, but maybe I'm expecting too much. Maybe she was just nervous about telling me she talked to Mason Redmond.

Mason Redmond is one of those names that can't be separated. I never just say "Mason" aloud. It's always "Mason Redmond." I'm not sure why certain names are like that and other names aren't. People just call me Remy. Only teachers and people reading names off a list call me Remy Boltuck.

Out of the corner of my eye, I see Mrs. Pursuit coming, and so we continue to work as we talk quietly. People come over to us and ask us questions about the contest. A frazzled mom of three little kids comes over, stressed that they hadn't signed up and worried if it's too late to enter.

Micayla finishes the last bag, and we start setting them up in a neat row. "So, let me tell you this story about Mason Redmond."

"Only if you admit that you actually like him," I insist.

"I don't know if I like him like that," Micayla says. "I'm still thinking about it."

"Whatever you say," I grumble.

We organize the bags and tidy up and then go sit on one of the benches by Dog Beach. We still have a few hours before the contest starts, and Bennett hasn't come back from putting up the signs.

"When you were watching Oscar, I just walked over to the volunteer table, and Mrs. Pursuit was panicking, and Mason was trying to calm her down, and he was reminding her that it always ends up being awesome." Micayla takes a deep breath. "Anyway, he just said, 'Hey, Micayla,' and I said, 'Hey, Mason,' and then we talked about how our names were kind of similar, and then he said you are really good with dogs."

"Me?" I gasp a little bit. Mason Redmond was talking about me? It's not like I really care, because I'm not the one with the crush on him. It's just surprising. I never think that anyone is talking about me.

"Yeah," Micayla says, in her no-big-deal tone. "Well, you are, Remy."

"Thanks." I smile, realizing we're off topic. "But what

about Mason Redmond? Do you like him or not?"

"I don't know," she says. "Okay, maybe I do. Today, I think I like him."

I have no idea what she means by *today*. But maybe it goes along with the saying to take things one day at a time. Maybe the person who first said it was dealing with a crush and unsure what to do.

We all go home to change, and I tell Bennett and Micayla that I'll meet them outside my house at five thirty so we can walk over to the beach together.

When Micayla and Bennett come to pick me up, they're laughing about something. When I ask them what it is, Bennett tells me it's some joke that Calvin heard, and they couldn't stop cracking up about it. I didn't ask what the joke was, because I don't really like Calvin, and I figured I wouldn't like the joke.

We get to the beach and Mrs. Pursuit tells us to stand behind the supply table. She hands us the sea-green SEA-GATE SANDCASTLE CONTEST 2014 shirts. Micayla and I had put on ribbed tank tops, because we knew we'd have to put the contest T-shirts on over them. Bennett did not, so he has to take his shirt off. Obviously this isn't a big deal, since he's a guy and guys go shirtless all the time at the beach, but I laugh anyway, and his face turns bright red.

I see him shirtless at the beach all the time, but it looks so funny to me when we're not standing on the sand about to jump into the ocean.

There are ten teams participating and lots of space for anyone who wants to sit and watch. People have been waiting all day for this, staying on the beach since early this morning just so they'd get a good seat.

One of the teams is made up of all the band members from Saturday We Tennis, and I have a feeling they're going to win. They won last year and a few years before that too.

A few of the teams are families with little kids, the way that Mom, Dad, Grandma, and I used to participate. We'd even let Danish help. He'd make cool imprints with his paws, and we always said that was the finishing touch. Memories of him are all over Seagate Island, and even when I'm not feeling entirely sad, something reminds me of him and I get filled with a flash of sadness again, like when the waves wash over your feet really quickly and then disappear moments later.

With a few minutes to go before the contest starts, I see Mr. Brookfield coming over to us, with Calvin and Claire tagging along behind.

I'm happy to see Mr. Brookfield but not the other two. Something about them makes me nervous and defensive. They're always criticizing Seagate, and it hurts. When you love a place so much, you can't stand to hear even one negative word about it. It was already different enough here without Danish by my side, and now these two come out of nowhere, complain about everything, and make the summer feel shaky.

Calvin and Claire don't even stay for the contest. They tell Bennett they're going over to the pool to swim and lie in the sun. But Mr. Brookfield stays.

I watch him in the distance a little bit, sitting on a bench, reading some kind of science fiction novel. He doesn't look happy, but he doesn't look sad either. I think about what it must have been like to finally get that part in the movie, only for it to kind of disappear, and there wasn't much he could do about it.

Mrs. Pursuit runs up to us, a whistle hanging around her neck and her frizzy brown hair in a high ponytail. She looks like an elderly middle school student, if that even makes any sense. "You all ready?" she asks us.

"I have an idea," I tell her. Micayla looks at me, confused, but I continue anyway. "Mr. Brookfield is totally famous—his voice is the scream in so many movies I'm sure you've seen. What if he does his scream into your megaphone to start the contest?"

I turn around to see if Mr. Brookfield hears what I'm saying, but he's too far away. Then it occurs to me that I probably should have asked him if he even wanted to do this.

"Do screams and sandcastles really go together?" Mrs. Pursuit asks us. "Let's think about it for next year."

I turn back again to check on Mr. Brookfield, and I notice that he's dozed off on the bench.

Well, Mrs. Pursuit did say we could think about it, so that's something. I'll have to find the right time to suggest it to Mr. Brookfield, and then we'll have a whole year to make it happen next summer. Maybe there are other ways to get his scream involved in Seagate life.

But it's such a peaceful place. No one screams here usually.

The teams have an hour to build their sandcastles, and they can have as many supplies as they want. Micayla and I are in charge of manning the supply table, in case anyone needs extra shovels or pails or cool sculpting devices.

At the last minute, the person who does all the photography for Seagate events had to cancel. Mrs. Pursuit bought disposable cameras at the general store and asked Bennett if he'd be willing to take some pictures. Of course, Bennett was thrilled to do it, and even from up here, I can see him running along the sand trying to get some great action shots of teams building their sandcastles.

So Micayla and I sit at the table, not really talking. I try to think of things to say, but everything seems wrong. I don't know why I'm having to think about things to say to her. This has never happened before.

"Bennett seems different this summer," I say, finally. It's been on my mind for weeks, but I haven't really had the courage to bring it up.

"Really?" Micayla asks, and I immediately want to take it back. I feel silly for even mentioning it.

"I guess he just seems to want to hang out with Calvin more than I thought he would," I say. "Know what I mean?"

She puts her feet up on the support beam in the folding table. "I guess so. Maybe. He's just Bennett." She hands a white shovel to a little kid who's all out of breath from running over the sand. "I haven't thought about it."

I ponder this for a few seconds. Is it new for me to think about Bennett this much? Maybe I didn't used to think about him at all. I wonder when this really started, and when it will stop. I wonder if there's anything I can do about it.

I drop the subject. Then Micayla spends forever telling me this story about her brother and how his bus broke down on the way back from Washington, DC, and he ended up spending the night at the house of someone he met on the bus. It's not really that interesting a story, but the way Micayla tells it, it sounds like a plot to some crazy movie.

Things start to feel more normal between us.

The Saturday We Tennis team wins the contest, and everyone runs down to see their sandcastle. They built it to look like a town house—tall, with square windows and a steep front stoop.

The Seagate Sandcastle Contest has loose rules—it's not limited to only traditional castles. All kinds of homes are acceptable. And that's what makes it different.

When the contest is over, Micayla, Bennett, and I walk

home together. After Micayla and Bennett drop me off, I think more about the fact that I guess I am thinking about Bennett. And I know that sounds totally crazy—thinking about thinking about something.

Over dinner, my parents can tell I'm acting a little strange, because they keep asking me if there's something on my mind.

I don't want to tell them about Bennett, though. It just doesn't feel like the kind of conversation you have with your parents.

The next morning, Micayla, Bennett, and I meet at Oscar's house. It makes me laugh that we think of it as his house instead of Dawn's house or her husband's house or even the babies' house. But the truth is, we know Oscar better than we know any of the others.

We know that Oscar likes to sit with us for a few minutes before we go out. I know we're not exactly having a conversation, but it almost feels like we're catching each other up on what has happened overnight or in some cases over the past few hours. We sit on the couch, Oscar sits in front of us, and we take turns petting him. His breathing slows down when we do this, and he looks so relaxed. It could be the way the white part of his fur curves, but I swear he even has a smile on his furry face.

After a few minutes of that, Oscar sips his water, we pack

up some treats in a little Tupperware container, and we head out. We leave Dawn either asleep on the couch or dealing with at least one crying baby.

We may leave with a calm Oscar, but we never leave a calm Dawn behind (unless she's asleep). And she always thanks us a million times.

Even though Micayla didn't start out as one of Oscar's dog sitters, she's quickly become his favorite. Maybe he can sense that she has allergies, so she stays back a little, and that's what makes him more attached to her. Whatever it is, Oscar loves Micayla, and when he's around, Micayla doesn't even really mind sneezing so much.

We have the same routine every day. We walk down to the boardwalk and then head over to Dog Beach, where Oscar plays with his friends, usually dogs that are much smaller than he is.

When we first started bringing him to the beach, he usually ignored Snowball and Marshmallow, but now they get along really well. They always chase each other at the beginning, and then when it seems like they need a break, they lie down in a circle with their paws in the middle facing each other.

They're a little crew who seem to pretty much ignore all the other dogs around them. Marshmallow and Snowball are smaller and daintier, kind of like Micayla and me. Oscar is bigger and more outgoing, like Bennett.

I watch them from across the sand, and I swear they're

even starting to look like us. I've heard that people can start to look like their dogs, but this may be taking it a bit too far—they're not even our dogs!

"Oscar is so kind," Micayla says. "Don't you see how he's always looking out for the other dogs? That black Lab just fell down and Oscar went to check on him."

"He's awesome," Bennett adds. "He seems like the camp counselor at the dog park, always going around to make sure the other dogs are having fun."

Just then Amber rushes up to us and taps me on the shoulder. "Hi, Remy, so sorry to barge in on you, but your mom said you were here. Would you mind keeping an eye on Marilyn Monroe for a second?" She smiles at me and then turns to face Micayla. "I'm not sure who is more inquisitive, my dog or my toddler! I guess my toddler, because he's running away!" She says the last part as she chases Hudson down the beach.

I'm so happy to see Marilyn Monroe on a day other than Monday or Wednesday that I bend down and scoop her up into my arms and give her a million kisses. Today, she has a purple bow in her hair, and the light brown part of her fur is looking extra light, almost like she's been tanning.

It's my first time seeing Marilyn Monroe at Dog Beach, and she runs around wildly, faster than any of the other dogs, stopping every five seconds to smell a section of sand or to study the dog closest to her. At Dog Beach, Marilyn Monroe has a constant expression of contentment. It seems like she's about to say, "This is nice. I'll take it," every time she stops moving.

I guess Oscar notices me by another dog, so he runs over and sits at our feet.

"Hi, Oscie," I say. "Are you jealous?"

He stands up on his back legs and scratches his paw against the top of my jean shorts. I pet him for a little while, and Bennett gives Marilyn Monroe some attention. Soon, Micayla comes over with the Maltese twins, and before I realize what's going on, we're in a circle surrounded by dogs.

We look like a magazine advertisement for dog food.

"Guys, look at us!" I yell. "We are surrounded by dogs." I'm not really a yeller, but between the barking and the sounds of the ocean, I'm forced to raise my voice.

"We must look crazy," Micayla shouts.

"We should start a doggie day camp," Bennett suggests. "Like Seagate Day Camp, but for dogs! Look, they love us!"

First Mr. Brookfield said it, and now Bennett, and the more we talk about it, the more I wish it was a real idea and not just a funny thing to think about.

We start coming up with all the activities we could do in our doggie day camp—totally in a joking way—but even discussing it is so much fun. We decide we could even safely offer instructional swim in the ocean, since dogs are already good swimmers. And we could serve lunch on Dog Beach.

"It'll be better than the Seagate Day Camp lunch," Bennett says. "We were practically eating dog food to begin with!"

Seagate Day Camp used to have a cook named Trey Fischer, and my mom said he was some musician back in the day. He loved cooking—he just wasn't very good at it. His lunches were pretty terrible. He somehow found a way to ruin grilled cheese. Eventually he retired, and now kids bring their lunches from home. It's much better that way.

"Thank you guys so much," Amber says, now pushing Hudson in a jogging stroller as he shoves Cheerios into his mouth. All parents have jogging strollers on Seagate—they're the only ones tough enough to maneuver on the sand. "Come on, Mari," Amber says. But Marilyn Monroe just stays where she is, lying on the sand, with Micayla rubbing her belly.

"Well, this is the happiest I've seen her since we've gotten to Seagate, except when she's with you, Remy," Amber admits. "Normally she has a dog walker in the city, since I have my hands full with this one." She points to the stroller. "I think she's felt neglected."

Wow. There really is a need for a doggie support group. All these dog owners admit that their dogs aren't getting the attention they need.

"Everyone loves Dog Beach," I admit. "Even humans."

Amber attempts to put Marilyn Monroe in the second seat in the stroller, and Bennett bursts out laughing. I elbow him to get him to stop, but in all fairness, it's just so funny. Soon Micayla is laughing too, and once two of us are cracking up, the third one can't help but laugh.

"It's crazy, I know." Amber is laughing along with us now.

"I should let her walk, but I need to get home quickly."

She puts Marilyn Monroe in the seat, only for her to hop back out. This happens three or four times, and then Amber turns to us. "Hey, I have a wacky idea. You guys can totally say no. I know this isn't in your set hours, but, Remy, you are so good with her. And you're here anyway. Do you have any interest in keeping an eye on her for a little while longer? And then walking her home?" She raises her eyebrows. "I'd pay you extra, of course."

The three of us look at each other, moving our eyebrows up and down, doing weird blinking patterns, trying to communicate with our eyes.

"Sure!" we all say at the same time.

"Thank you." Amber smiles. "I had a feeling Remy would have awesome friends."

We spend another hour at Dog Beach, playing with the dogs, running around with them, and joking that we're on the path to really running a doggie day camp.

After that, we return Oscar to Dawn, and Marilyn Monroe to Amber, and we tell them that we're available for walks in the afternoon if they need us.

"So you're making all this dog-watching money," Bennett says to me as we're walking home. "Are you saving up for something?"

I shrug. "I haven't thought about it really."

"Well, there's a new iPhone coming out in September; you can always get that," Micayla suggests.

"Maybe." It does sound cool, but I feel weird taking these people's money, since I enjoy watching the dogs and spending time with them so much. In some ways, I feel like I should be paying *them*. Spending time with these pups has helped me so much when I'm sad and missing Danish. It's not like he's been replaced, but spending time with other dogs is better than spending time without any dogs at all. In the back of my mind, I've already decided that I'm going to donate the money to an animal shelter in Manhattan when we get home.

We're all so tired after the morning of dog-sitting that we head down to the pool and get side-by-side lounge chairs and decide to pull a Mr. Brookfield and take an afternoon nap right out in the open.

"Psst," I hear Micayla say, from the lounge chair next to me.

"I'm sleeping," I mumble, even though I know that won't stop Micayla from talking. We made a pact at a sleepover when we were eight that we could always wake each other up if we had something to say. And we've never broken that pact.

"Do you think it's weird that people trust us so much with their dogs?" she whispers.

"No, they can tell we're dog people," I assure her. "Dog people can sense other dog people. It's kind of like how moms can tell if another woman is a mom too."

"Is that true?" Micayla asks.

"I think so."

"Okay," Micayla says, and closes her eyes again.

But after that, I'm pretty convinced my afternoon nap is over. I've never been much of a napper. My mom says that getting me to nap even as a baby was pretty difficult, that the only place I'd really nap was in the stroller on the boardwalk. Obviously this only worked in the summer months, so winter in New York City was kind of hard.

I look over at my two friends, sleeping peacefully on the beautiful royal blue lounge chairs, and I realize that though things may be different this summer—it's strange without Danish, and we didn't expect to be dog-sitting—maybe different is okay. Maybe I can get used to different.

16

After the pool, I'm home, sitting on the front porch with my mom, when Mr. Brookfield walks over and asks to talk to her. That's something about Seagate that's probably the most different thing of all—people rarely use the phone; they'll just walk to someone's house to talk to them. It's kind of like we're living in olden times, in a tiny village.

My mom walks with Mr. Brookfield over to the garden at the side of the house. I twist my head a little to move my ear as close to the conversation as possible.

"Their mother would like them to be more social," I hear Mr. Brookfield say. "I am doing what I can. Would Remy like to come over for pizza later?"

I can't help but smile. Mr. Brookfield is making plans for Calvin and Claire like they're little kids. I bet back in West-chester, they're super popular and always busy. But on

Seagate, if you're not happy, you're a little bit weird.

"It's fine with me, but maybe you'll just want to ask Remy on your way out?" I hear my mom say. I don't know what to do. I don't want to say yes if I don't know if Micayla and Bennett are going. I don't know Calvin and Claire that well, and they don't really seem to like me, so I wouldn't want to go alone. But I can't tell Mr. Brookfield that.

"Remy, my dear." Mr. Brookfield looks around for me. He pretty much calls everyone his dear, but it's still a nice thing to say. "Would you care to dine at Casa Brookfield this evening? We will be eating Seagate's finest pizza."

I smile. "I accept your invitation, Mr. Brookfield."

"She's so polite," he tells my mom, and then turns to me. "See you at six."

When we can't see Mr. Brookfield anymore, my mom says, "That was nice of you, Remy. He's hoping his grandchildren can make the most of their summer here."

"It doesn't seem like they try very hard," I grumble. "And Seagate isn't a place you have to make the most of. It's a place where you relish every second."

"That may be true for you, but what's true for you isn't true for everyone."

It is as far as I can see.

A few minutes later, Micayla and Bennett text that they're going over to Mr. Brookfield's too, and I immediately feel better. It won't be that bad. If you're eating slices from Seagate Pizzeria, you don't really have much to complain about.

★ ★ ★

At six, we all meet over there. I'm the first one to arrive, so Claire takes me up to her room and shows me some of the new jeans she got when she was home.

"These are called the Five-Pocket Rocket," she tells me. "I hope I'm the only one to have them when we start school."

"They're really nice," I say, not because I notice anything that special about them, but because she seems so happy and proud.

She puts that pair on her bed and takes another pair out of the pale pink shopping bag. "And these are the Toile Stamp. They're brand-new, but the lady at the jeans store said they're definitely the next big thing."

"I like the stitching on the pockets." It was all I could come up with. To me, jeans are jeans. I can't ever tell the difference.

"That's exactly why they're going to be such a big deal," Claire says, holding the jeans up in front of us. "The stitching is all hand-done, and each pair is a tiny bit different."

"I could tell," I say, feeling proud I noticed something special. Then, a second later, it feels weird to be proud of noticing something I don't care about, like jeans.

We hear the doorbell, and for a moment I'm disappointed. Claire and I were finally connecting. Sure, it was about something totally superficial, but I still felt good about it.

"My man! Bennett!" I hear Calvin say. I look over the second-floor railing as they greet each other. They slap a high five so loud that I'm sure it made their hands sting.

"Calvin!" Bennett yells, and they do this weird chest-bump thing. I've never seen Bennett like this. It's almost as if he's acting in a play.

As soon as he sees me, he straightens his shirt a little and starts talking in his normal voice again. Soon Micayla arrives, and we sit in Mr. Brookfield's backyard drinking lemonade and eating cookies.

"Here we eat dessert before dinner," Mr. Brookfield tells us. "It's kind of a house rule."

"My kind of rule," I add.

Bennett and Calvin play paddleball against the back of Mr. Brookfield's house, and Claire, Micayla, and I sit around, still talking about Claire's new jeans. It seems that if we're talking about what she wants to talk about, she's happy. That's probably not a good quality, but it's better than having her rain on everyone else's fun.

"Pizza delivery!" Mr. Brookfield walks into the backyard carrying five pizzas. I'm pretty sure he over-ordered. Bennett jumps up to help him, and I feel proud again, prouder than Claire was about her new jeans.

Bennett is a good person. So what if he talked in that crazy voice before? He's good. He always does the right thing. I watch him talking to Mr. Brookfield as they set up the pizza, and I realize something. It doesn't matter who you are—if Bennett is talking to you, you feel like you're the only person in the world.

We sit and eat our pizza on Mr. Brookfield's Adirondack chairs.

"Would anyone care for some nice music while you eat your dinner?" Mr. Brookfield asks.

"Put on that scream recording," I tell him.

"Yeah!" Micayla says.

"Seriously, guys." Claire makes a face at us. "No one wants to listen to someone screaming over and over again."

"We do," I say.

Bennett looks at Calvin. It seems like he's waiting to see what Calvin does before he says anything. Maybe they're not paying attention, though, because they both stand up for another slice. They've already finished a whole pizza, just the two of them.

Mr. Brookfield puts on the scream recording loud enough for us to hear it in the backyard but not so loud that those awful Spitzes hear it next door. Although maybe it would stop their bickering and bring a smile to their always-disgruntled faces.

"Tell us the story again," I say to Mr. Brookfield, and everyone groans, except Bennett. I know most people don't like to hear the same story over and over again, so I don't mind when the rest of them go inside to play some video game on the computer, and I stay outside with Mr. Brookfield.

"Mrs. Pursuit said that maybe next summer your scream could be the signal for the start of the Sandcastle Contest," I tell him.

"Ah, never thought of that," he says.

"We can find other ways to make your scream a part of the Seagate tradition," I say. "It doesn't just have to live in the recording forever."

He replies, "I don't mind it. Sometimes things stay in the past and that's okay."

"Really?"

"Sometimes, Remy." He pats me on the shoulder. "Now go on inside with everyone else. Calvin has been playing this video game nonstop. Maybe you can explain to me what the big deal is."

"I'll try."

Bennett and Calvin play the game for hours—or at least it seems that way—so Claire, Micayla, and I go back upstairs to look through Claire's closet.

"I'm glad you guys are so into fashion," she says, which makes me realize that maybe she's not all that into fashion herself. If she were, she'd probably be able to tell that we pretty much wear the same jean shorts every single day.

We're going through Claire's hooded sweatshirt collection (so far we've counted fifteen) when we hear stomping up the stairs. The boys come barging in.

I hear my phone beep three times, telling me I have a voice mail. I can't believe what it says.

"You guys," I say, a little out of breath. "I just got a call. Marilyn Monroe's mother recommended us to another dog owner."

"Marilyn Monroe's mother!" Claire yelps, and bursts out laughing.

"She's a dog," I explain.

"She's, like, a really famous, beautiful actress, Remy," Claire replies.

"Duh. I know that. But Marilyn Monroe is also the name of a dog on Seagate." I glare at her. "I watch her two mornings a week. She's my pal."

"When? What kind of dog?" Micayla asks, ignoring Claire.

Claire looks at us like we've all lost our minds and goes back to her closet. I wonder if she has any clothes left at home, or if she brought everything she owns to Seagate.

"A Newfoundland named Rascal," I tell them. "I don't know when. We have to call her back."

I look at my phone to make sure I save the message and see another missed call and a voice mail. A man needs help with his German shepherd named Atticus.

"Wow, are you guys, like, running a dog-sitting business or something?" Claire asks, folding what seems like her fifth gray hoodie.

"I guess so," the three of us reply at the same time.

Sometimes something that starts out small becomes another thing entirely. Watching one dog turned into watching many dogs. And maybe that's how Mr. Brookfield feels about his scream. To him, it's just a loud scream, but to movie watchers, it's a huge part of the experience.

Micayla, Bennett, and I agreed to meet at the Dollhouse Café for breakfast at eight in the morning. We want to beat the brunch crowd and be able to sit and talk about our plans for this dog-sitting business. When we first discussed a doggie day camp, we were kidding, but now that we're starting to get more requests, it really seems like it's happening.

Although I'm usually the latest sleeper of us all, I get to the Dollhouse Café before they do, which is great because it gives me a few minutes to look around and see if Fatima has added any new dollhouses to the place. She collects dollhouses, but she keeps them all at the restaurant so that everyone can see them. She even lets the kids play with them before their meal arrives or when they're done and waiting for their parents to finish. She has every kind of dollhouse—

old wooden ones, modern plastic ones, steep dollhouses like brownstones in Brooklyn, and sprawling mansions like you'd find in Victorian England.

The scrambled eggs here are the best in the world, and you get some time to play with a dollhouse—what could be better?

Fatima greets me with her famous "How are things?" and I tell her I'm meeting Micayla and Bennett here. She brings a basket of fresh muffins and scones and a hot chocolate.

"Sorry we're late," Bennett says when they get to the table.

We all order the same thing: scrambled eggs with cheddar and chives (Fatima's specialty), as well as buttered biscuits and home fries.

"Calvin was really intrigued by our business," Bennett tells us.

"Let's not declare it a business yet," Micayla adds. "We haven't even called the new clients back."

Micayla's usually a morning person, but she seems really grumpy today. She's slumped over in her chair, and her eyes are puffy, almost like she's been crying.

"Let's vote on a name first," Bennett says. "Things become real when they have a name, I think."

I take a second to ponder that, and I think he may be on to something. Maybe Mr. Brookfield's scream never became known because it didn't have a name. I wonder what would happen if we named it now.

"Sure," I say. "How about the Seagate Dog Sitters Service?"

"What about Seagate Pooch Pals?" Micayla suggests.

"Or Seagate Doggie Day Camp, like we said originally?" Bennett starts writing down the names on the place mat. I like how organized he is.

I sip my hot chocolate and say, "Y'know what? Let's think about it while we discuss all the other stuff first." If we're going to name it, it has to be the right name. And I'm just not sure we can come up with it on the spot.

They agree, and I go through all the other stuff that we need to discuss: calling back the people who have called us, making up a schedule of who handles what dog and when, putting up posters so we can get other customers, and making sure we always have bags to carry any supplies the dogs need and also to clean up after them.

"This is kind of a lot of work," Micayla admits.

"It'll be fine, Mic." I rub her shoulder. "We're in this together."

"What about me? I have to take care of Asher, and Calvin's trying to convince me to take this lifeguarding class with him at the pool. It starts in a few days." Bennett's phone starts ringing and he answers it right here, even though his mom hates it when people take calls in restaurants. "Yo, dude," he says. "Yeah, okay, I'll call you."

"Calvin?" I ask.

Bennett nods and goes back to his eggs. We divide up the customer calls and agree to meet at Oscar's around ten, when we always pick him up. The other dog owners can bring their pets to Dog Beach around ten thirty, and we can figure out their needs.

Bennett leaves early so he can go check out the sign-up sheet for the lifeguarding class. Then it's just Micayla and me, finishing our breakfast. Micayla keeps saying how overwhelming this dog-sitting thing is and how she didn't expect to have a job this summer. I need to change the topic, because she's starting to make me feel stressed. The thing is, I don't understand why she's suddenly so crazed with all of it.

Everyone was so excited yesterday. I don't understand what happened.

"So what else is new?" I ask her. I realize this sounds so dumb, since I spend pretty much all day with her, every day, but I wanted to change the topic.

"Huh?"

"I mean, like, I dunno, have you heard from your home friends? Did you get your last report card? Who are your teachers going to be next year?" I look down at my plate. It suddenly feels strange to make eye contact with her.

She moves her chair back from the table a little bit. "My stomach is starting to hurt." She takes a sip of water. "You're asking me too many questions."

We're the kind of friends who can always be honest with each other, but I wish she hadn't said that. No one likes someone who's pushy and makes them nervous. Maybe I did ask too many questions.

I stay quiet and finish my muffin and try to think of something funny to say, but nothing comes to me. When you're friends like Micayla and I are friends, you can usually read each other's mind. But I guess I messed up.

I look into Micayla's hot chocolate mug. "Yours looks creamier than mine."

"I think I got an extra marshmallow."

Micayla and I used to do this all the time when we were little—compare our hot chocolates, count the marshmallows in each mug, see how the color changed as we drank it. I don't know why we did it, or how it started, or why it was even a game, but somehow it made drinking the hot chocolate even tastier.

That's pretty much how everything is with Micayla—she makes every game more fun, every meal more delicious.

I think back to what Mr. Brookfield said about thinking about the past too much, and how it's important to also focus on the present and the future. But the past is comforting, and the future seems overwhelming.

Focusing on the present is probably most important anyway. And that's good, because we have a lot to focus on with this new dog-sitting business. It may not have a name yet, but it has a ton of potential.

"You guys might want to hand out a form," Mason Redmond tells us. We're all standing around Dog Beach, watching Oscar and waiting for our other clients to show up. It sounds silly to refer to dogs as clients, but I'm not sure what else to call them.

"Like for the owners to fill out, with the dog's name, their owner's number, any special information you might need to know," he continues. "Or I guess you could put it all in your phones."

"That's a genius idea!" Micayla yelps. "Save paper, and we'll have it handy! With a folder, we could forget it or lose it or something, but we guard our phones with our lives." I'm glad to hear her enthusiastic again, after our awkward breakfast at the Dollhouse Café. Maybe she was just having a bad morning.

Bennett laughs. "That's kind of embarrassing to admit, Mic."

"It's just society these days," Mason adds, like he's some old grandfather and not a kid who is exactly our age. "We're so focused on technology and disconnected from—"

"Well, thanks for the advice, Mason," I interrupt him, because he'll go on and on about something for hours, and I see Marilyn Monroe coming.

"From now on, can you please pick her up?" Amber asks us, looking exhausted. "I'll pay extra; I just can't schlep her here and then schlep Hudson to music class."

I want to remind her that the whole island is only five miles long and seven miles wide, but I don't think that would really help her much. Plus, I'm used to her frazzled state of mind. I feel really good when I can calm her down and make her feel better.

"Amber, we're going to be taking on some new clients, so we're reorganizing our schedule," I tell her. "We should be able to pick up Marilyn Monroe. By the time we return her to you, we'll let you know how the rest of the week will go."

She smiles and looks down at her stroller to see her sleeping toddler. "Thank you for being so organized." She sighs. "Guess we missed Seagate Toddler Jam. But at least I can sit outside and enjoy my coffee in peace."

Amber leaves and Marilyn Monroe runs around happily, her red bow in her hair just perfectly. Oscar comes over to greet her, and they bark at each other for a few minutes.

I'm starting to get the sense that Oscar may have a crush on Marilyn Monroe—it's the way he follows her around but doesn't get too close, and the way he looks for her all the time, even when he's not with her.

It's like Micayla and Mason Redmond.

Rascal and Atticus arrive a few minutes later, even though the owners don't seem to know each other. The woman who brings Rascal is wearing yoga pants and a tank top and keeps running in place even as she talks to us. "I'm Andi, nice to meet you." She smiles. "Rascal is my mother's dog, but she's recovering from a hip replacement and can't walk much now," Andi says, panting in a similar fashion to Rascal. I notice this and cover my mouth to stop myself from cracking up. "So, if you could pick him up and watch him for a few hours, and then bring him back to 328 Seashell Place, that would be great. I teach yoga and have a very busy schedule."

"We can handle that," Micayla says, petting Rascal's head.

"Great. Thanks."

Micayla puts Andi's information into her phone while I introduce myself to Rascal. His fur is so smooth and silky and as black as can be—it looks like velvet. He's happy digging in the sand, but before we know it, he's off and running and swimming in the water. We get a little freaked out at first, but Mason assures us that Newfoundlands are good swimmers.

Atticus's owner stays around for a little while and plays with him, and then he tells us that Atticus appears lonely at home and needs to make some friends. "I don't know what it is," the man tells us. "I just get the vibe that he's bored."

We turn around and watch Atticus sprinting across the sand and into the water and playing with Rascal. It almost looks like they're purposely splashing each other.

"Are you on Seagate all summer?" I ask. "What's his life like at home?"

Bennett cracks up and elbows me. "You sound like my mom, Rem! You can be a doggie psychiatrist."

I start laughing too, and even Atticus's owner chuckles a bit.

"I'm a literature professor, and we rented a house for the summer, just Atticus and me, but I'm busy working on my new book," he tells us. "I'm Paul, by the way."

We all introduce ourselves, and I start to wonder—is Atticus lonely? Or is Paul the lonely one?

Are all owners' problems reflected in their dogs?

I'm too embarrassed to say any of this out loud, but maybe Paul should be bringing Atticus here to meet other dog owners, and they'd both make friends.

"How'd you find out about us, Paul?"

"My neighbor is Amber, Marilyn Monroe's owner."

We nod.

"She mentioned some kids who were watching dogs, and I figured it would be good for Atti."

Atticus and Rascal hit it off right away, almost as if they've been waiting their whole lives to meet and be friends. I start to wonder if the yoga lady and Paul would make good friends too.

Bennett, Micayla, and I finish putting the dogs' names and owners' contact information into our phones, and we spend the next few hours running and playing with them.

Marilyn Monroe usually sits and waits for other dogs to come to her. She likes to hang with me, and sometimes I think she's asking me to go to Daisy's, just the two of us, like we did that one time. I get that sad, missing-Danish feeling, but I don't have much time to feel bad. I'm hanging out with four dogs right now, and my best friends.

I'll always miss Danish, but I can't think about it all the time.

Oscar is the kind of dog who hangs out with everyone, checking on Marilyn Monroe every few minutes, visiting the Maltese duo, swimming with Atticus and Rascal every now and then.

It's only been a few hours, but all the doggie personalities are coming through.

I sit back on the bench for a few minutes and take it all in. We actually have a dog-sitting business. We still have to set our prices, but I almost don't care if we get paid.

It seems so strange and so amazing, I don't even know what to really think about it.

Off to one side, I see Micayla talking to Mason Redmond. They're actually chatting and she's not running away. I see Oscar going up to Marilyn Monroe every few minutes, and it's seriously cute, but I wonder if she's starting to get annoyed. She turns away from him every now and again.

I look around for Bennett and see him throwing a Frisbee to Rascal, while Atticus tries to get into the game too.

Bennett talks to them like they're people, not dogs. "Atticus, hold up a minute, pal."

I'm watching them and Bennett doesn't notice, so I keep watching and laughing as Rascal brings the Frisbee back over and over again, and Atticus jumps up on Bennett's legs to get it out of his hand.

Bennett's cargo shorts are hanging low, and he keeps pulling them up. He's wearing the T-shirt from last year's Seagate Sandcastle Contest, and I don't know what it is exactly, or why it's happening now, but I feel like I'm seeing Bennett, my Bennett, my best friend for life, in this whole new way. Like all the times I saw him before, it was a blur, or I didn't look closely enough, or I didn't notice him at all.

It's like the narrow wooden table in the foyer of our Seagate house. It's been there forever, and I never paid any attention to it. But the other day I lost my keys and I was searching everywhere. I discovered they had fallen and were underneath that wooden table.

I was so grateful to find the keys that I looked at the table more closely and realized it has all these pretty designs on it. My mom told me that Grandma and Grandpa found it lying on the sidewalk one day. They brought it in, cleaned it up, and then carved their initials in the bottom—MB + SB.

It had been in our house all this time, and I never knew that.

Bennett feels like that table right now, only better and more special and more lovable.

I want to run up to him and tell him that, tell him the whole thing about the table, because I really think he'd understand. But I can't. I'm worried the words would come out weird, and I wouldn't make any sense.

So I stay back on the bench and continue to take it all in.

It doesn't take long for us to settle into a schedule.

I go pick up Marilyn Monroe and Atticus, since they live on the same street and they're the closest to me. Micayla picks up Rascal, and Bennett picks up Oscar, and we all meet at Daisy's before we walk over to Dog Beach.

On the days that I watch Hudson and hang with Marilyn Monroe in the mornings, Micayla and Bennett take care of the other dogs and then we meet them there.

Sometimes we get pancakes at Daisy's, and the dogs spend time together, drinking water and eating treats. Sometimes we just pick up lemonades to go.

Either way, it's a routine. And I like routine.

The days speed by, taking care of the dogs—we're with them every weekday morning and sometimes afternoons too. We also have a few new clients.

Buttercup, the yellow Lab, is here for the next two weeks. She's part of a family with two parents and two kids, and they're always taking day trips. They go to explore the lighthouses on all the islands and also take ferry trips to Connecticut and Massachusetts. So when they're on a day trip, we get Buttercup for the whole day. She's sweet and playful and is just the friend Marilyn Monroe needed.

When Buttercup's not with us, we can all tell that Marilyn Monroe misses her. She'll wander around aimlessly, looking forlorn. We give her extra treats on those days.

We also watch a Shar-Pei named Lucky every now and again. He's only on Seagate for another week, but his owners like to spend all day sunbathing and reading on the beach. Lucky pretty much keeps to himself, but Bennett's trying to get him to come out of his shell.

Every time I see Bennett, I get this excited, energetic feeling. It's so weird. I was always excited to see him, but now it's different, and I can't even really explain it or understand it. I keep thinking it's going to disappear, but it's almost the end of July and it's still here. A month from now, we'll be leaving Seagate, and I have no idea what I'll do with this feeling when I won't see Bennett every day.

We're so busy taking care of the dogs, but we still have time for fun. The Seagate Knowbodies Trivia Competition is tomorrow, and I can't wait. It's definitely on my list of top five favorite nights of the summer.

Micayla, Bennett, and I are always a team, and we compete against other teams of three. The teams can be all kids or all adults, and everyone is treated fairly. Some people think it's weird for kids to compete against adults, but when it comes to Seagate Trivia, sometimes the kids know more.

We've won the past two years in a row, and I think we can win this year too.

Mr. Brookfield invites us over for pizza again, and I hope we'll have time to go over our trivia after dinner. I don't want to talk about it too much in front of Calvin and Claire, though, because I don't want to make them feel bad about not being on our team.

We've been to Mr. Brookfield's for pizza once a week for the last three weeks. He always orders too much, puts dessert out first, and pretends he doesn't want to play his scream recording, when I know he really does.

Calvin and Claire seem to have warmed up to life on Seagate, even though they don't really do much except lie by the pool and eat ice cream. They haven't asked to help with the dogs, and we haven't offered.

The way things are going, business could get really crazy in August, though, and we may need to ask for their help. We'll see. I'm getting along with Claire a little better now, but I wouldn't want her to say something mean and ruin the dog-sitting.

We're all sitting around eating our pizza, listening to the Scream, when I overhear Bennett and Calvin talking.

"Did you tell them yet?" Calvin whispers to Bennett, and

then looks up. He sees me looking at them, and I guess he knows I overheard.

I can't help it. I look at Bennett way more than I used to.

"No, man." Bennett bites into his slice. "I will. Don't worry."

Calvin nudges Bennett, and then they both look up at me, and now they both know I was listening. I look down at my plate and pretend to be really involved in whatever Micayla and Claire are discussing.

"Yeah, my mom says I have to wait until eighth grade to wear makeup to school," Claire says. "But no one really wears it yet where I live anyway. Just, like, a little lip gloss."

"Same with me," Micayla adds.

"What are you guys talking about?" I ask.

"Shh," Micayla says to Claire, not to me, and I can't figure out what's going on. What's so secret about wearing makeup?

I decide not to ask questions, but it bothers me the whole rest of the night. We end up staying at Mr. Brookfield's really late, and we don't have time to practice our trivia.

"Don't worry. We know everything there is to know about Seagate," Micayla tells me as we're walking home. "They don't change the questions much."

I shrug. "I guess so."

"I have to tell you guys something," Bennett says, following a few steps behind us out of Mr. Brookfield's house.

I had almost forgotten about Bennett and Calvin's secret conversation. What with Micayla and Claire's weird makeup talk, there are too many secrets and strange whispers to keep track of.

"What?" I ask.

"Promise you won't be mad," Bennett says. He smiles a little in his goofy, cheerful Bennett way, and I feel like I could never be mad at him, no matter what. But I'd never tell him that.

"What is it?" Micayla asks, impatient.

"I'll be here for Seagate Knowbodies, but I have to bail on the next few days of dog-sitting," he tells us. It's a short sentence, but it feels like a knife in my chest, and I'm not sure why. "Calvin invited me to go on his dad's boat for a few days, and I feel like I should go."

"Well, don't go just because you feel like you should," I say, and then instantly regret it. I sound angry and I don't like it.

"No, um, I mean . . ." Bennett waits a few seconds before talking again. "I want to go. I think it'll be cool. Just us guys."

I don't know what to say to that.

"It's okay for me to have other friends, you know." He jabs me a little with his elbow, like he's joking. But sometimes jokes can be truths in disguise. I think this is one of those times.

"No biggie," Micayla says, like none of what Bennett said was a big deal or even a little bit surprising. "Rem and I can handle the pooches."

We get to her house, and she says good night and blows

us kisses, the way she always does. Through the window, we see her mom sitting in the big armchair, reading.

Maybe Micayla doesn't think it's a big deal that Bennett's leaving for a few days, but I do. I know I can't say that, though. I know I need to play it cool and act like it's fine. I mean, of course it's fine. Bennett can have other friends.

I just don't know why it feels so sad. It's not like he's going on the boat trip and never coming back.

"We'll be fine with the dogs," I say. I realize that we passed by Bennett's house, and he kept walking with us until he finished talking, and now he's walking me home, totally out of his way.

"You'll be more than fine," Bennett says. "You're awesome with those dogs, Rem."

"Thanks. But you are too." I smile. "Imagine, if you never found Oscar, we might not even have this business."

He shakes his head. "Imagine if you never started sitting at Amber's house while Hudson napped. And you were the one who cared about finding Oscar in the first place." He high-fives me, and I walk down the stone path to my house.

When I get to the door, I can't resist looking back at him. "Get psyched for trivia," I say. He's just standing there, at the end of the path, watching me walk inside. I wonder what that means. I've never seen him do that before.

"You know it," he replies.

20

The next day is really busy. We meet at Dog Beach earlier than usual because Oscar's mom has to take the babies to their pediatrician. I get worried that he'll be lonely without Marilyn Monroe and the others, so all the dogs get picked up early.

Then we take them for lunch at Daisy's—she serves up a full doggie menu on weekdays, when she's not so busy—and we entertain them for most of the afternoon.

I can tell that Marilyn Monroe wishes it was just the two of us at Daisy's, the way she sits on my lap at the table and then leaves a few dog treats by my feet, as if she thinks I'd enjoy the treats too.

It's a great day, but by the end, we're so tired that I'm worried we won't have enough energy for trivia.

"Let's meet there," Micayla tells me as we're walking home

from Sundae Best. After such a tiring day, we deserve ice cream and we need the sugar to energize ourselves. "Six o'clock, right?"

I nod. Bennett's already back home, since he needed to meet Asher after camp. I don't know why they wouldn't pick me up on the way, but I'm too tired to ask.

I rush inside, shower, put on a pair of skinny jeans and a tank top—and even though I only planned to lie down for five minutes, I fall sound asleep on my bed.

When I wake up and look at my clock, it's five thirty.

I rush out of bed, tie my hair back in a ponytail, since it's such a mess from my falling asleep with it wet, and hurry downstairs.

"Rem, no dinner?" my mom asks. She grilled some hot dogs, and they're on a platter in the middle of the kitchen table.

"I can't. Seagate Knowbodies tonight."

"Take a hot dog for the walk," my mom says. "We'll meet you there."

I quickly put a hot dog on a paper plate, squirt some ketchup on it, and hurry out the door.

I get there in ten minutes, and I'm pretty impressed with my ability to walk and eat. Micayla and Bennett are already sitting up on the stage, and they're testing out the buzzers. The best part of Seagate Knowbodies (aside from winning) is that we get to use actual buzzers like in a real game show.

"Sorry I'm late, guys," I say, a little out of breath.

Micayla motions to me that I have something on my face, and I quickly wipe away the drop of ketchup from the corner of my mouth. Maybe I'm not as good at walking and eating as I thought I was.

I sit between Micayla and Bennett. They saved me the middle seat. It was nice of them to do that, but that wasn't the reason they did it. They did it because we always sit in this order, and we're a little superstitious. We've won the past two years sitting in this exact formation.

Up on the stage, I can see everything. All the people who came to watch, Sundae Best's ice cream cone sign, the one-dollar-books cart in front of Novel Ideas Book Shop, and even the path all the way to the ocean.

They only put up the stage a few times a year: for Seagate Knowbodies, for the Fourth of July concert, and for the judges of the Seagate Halloween Costume Contest.

I feel lucky that I get to sit here, because the view is one of the best in the world.

Unfortunately, I also see Claire and Calvin in the front row. Yes, they have grown on me, but it doesn't feel right to see them at such a Seagate-y event. Also, Calvin is sitting there making faces at Bennett, doing those armpit farts and then pretending to faint from the imaginary smell. He's going to distract Bennett, and we're going to lose. I don't think that's what any of us want. And Claire looks ridiculously bored, staring at her phone and rolling her eyes.

"Welcome to the fifteenth annual Seagate Knowbodies

Trivia Competition!" Mr. Aprone yells out into his megaphone. He's the head of the Seagate Community Association, and he also owns the Novel Ideas Book Shop. He lives in Rhode Island but comes to Seagate every weekend of the year. "That's K-N-O-W, people! Our reigning champions, Team RemBenMic, are back, and we also have a few newcomers, Team Sunny Days and Team No Sugar Added."

We're allowed to keep coming back to the contest because we keep winning, but the newcomers have to go through a rigorous selection process. They have to submit a proposal about why they want to participate, and they have to score high enough on Mr. Aprone's entrance exam. He takes this whole thing very seriously, obviously, which only makes it more fun.

"Team No Sugar Added is a group of ladies from the diabetes support group," Micayla whispers to me. Her mom is a nurse and she volunteers with that group during the summer, helping answer questions and stuff. "They look so excited, don't they?"

"Yeah." I look over at them again after I hear the loud slaps from their high fives. "I guess they're not Sundae Best's best customers." I laugh.

"They have sugar-free flavors," Micayla reminds me, all serious-sounding. Maybe my joke wasn't really that funny.

"So, teams, hands off the buzzers!" Mr. Aprone says. "We're ready to begin."

He pauses for applause, and I see Calvin standing up,

clapping furiously, the only one who has decided to give us a standing ovation before the contest has even started.

Bennett cracks up but stops when I glare at him.

"First question: How many gazebos are there on Seagate?"

My hand hits the buzzer first. Mr. Aprone always starts with an easy one, and this one is almost too easy.

"Yes, RemBenMic has hit the buzzer first," he says. He has a screen that shows which team's buzzer buzzes first, so there's really no debating it.

"Six," I answer.

"That is correct," Mr. Aprone says. "Bonus question goes to RemBenMic first and then will be opened to the other teams if they answer incorrectly. It is: Where are the gazebos located?"

I don't have to hit the buzzer since it's our question, but I do offer it up to Micayla and Bennett to see if they want to answer. They shake their heads. Maybe I'm imagining it, but I start to feel like I'm the only one fired up about the contest.

"On the grassy lawn by the stadium, by the entryway to West Beach, one in front of Sundae Best, one by the entrance to Dog Beach, one behind High Tide Bar & Grill, and one at the end of Ocean Walk."

"That is correct!"

Everyone claps after I answer, and even Claire looks a little bit proud, but Bennett and Micayla have sort of a delayed reaction. They don't look as excited as they should be. I want to nudge them with my elbow and get them to perk up. I wonder if it's the long day with the dogs that exhausted them, or if it's something else. I can't interrupt the contest to ask.

I also can't be the only one on the team to answer the questions. That's a Seagate Knowbodies rule—one team member can answer a maximum of three questions in a row.

"Next question," Mr. Aprone says after he adjusts his microphone. It was making a terrible screeching sound, and we all had to cover our ears. "When was Seagate founded?"

I attempt to hit the buzzer, but No Sugar Added gets to it first. I guess I delayed a little bit because I was hoping Micayla or Bennett would take the chance.

"1932," one of the women answers.

The bonus question is who was the first person to come to Seagate, and of course I know the answer is Melvin Jasper, but they get the first chance to answer and they get it right.

The next question goes to Sunny Days, but I didn't know the answer. It was some geographic question about what it's called when an ocean experiences two equal high tides and two equal low tides in a day. The answer is *semidiurnal*, and I always forget that.

We each get a few more questions, and then the score is tied.

"Come on, guys," I say, finally. Micayla did get the answer right about the number of kids in Seagate Schoolhouse's first graduating class, so I high-fived her for that. "We need to perk up! Bennett, you haven't answered a single question."

"Okay, okay." He does this weird finger signal to Calvin and then bursts out laughing. It seems like Bennett would much rather be in the audience watching with Calvin instead of participating with us. "The next one is all me."

So when Mr. Aprone asks, "Name the famous actor who once had a summer home on Seagate," and Bennett hits the buzzer, I get all excited because he obviously knows this one.

Except that when Bennett's ready to answer, Calvin does some awkward fist-bump thing and Bennett starts laughing and then says, "Alec Baldwin."

"Unfortunately, that's incorrect," Mr. Aprone says.

Then No Sugar Added hits the buzzer because I'm not allowed to answer, since my teammate got it wrong.

"George Clooney," one of the ladies says, and that team takes the lead.

"That is correct!" Mr. Aprone yells. "We will now take a five-minute break."

"Bennett!" I say. "Don't you remember our moms telling us the story over and over again?"

He looks at me, confused.

"Remember? When we were little babies, I was crying so loud that George Clooney came over from his table at Picnic to our table and picked me up and got me to quiet down?"

"Why were you eating at Picnic when you were so little?" he asks me.

"My parents' anniversary." I glare at him. That's so not the important part of the story. What is wrong with him? "Duh."

"Sorry, Rem." He hits the buzzer accidentally and gets everyone's attention. "Sorry, folks, technical difficulties." He's not even making sense. That wasn't a technical difficulty; that was him being stupid, but Calvin laughs anyway.

It seems Calvin will laugh at whatever Bennett does.

He's ruining our chances at winning for the third year in a row, and yet he's just laughing. I turn my head to whisper something to Micayla, and I notice that she's not sitting next to me anymore.

I look around, shocked that I didn't even notice her leaving. Maybe she was sick and had to leave in a hurry. I wonder if I should go check on her. Then I look out into the audience and I see her sitting next to Avery Sanders, whispering something in her ear.

Mr. Aprone announces that the break is over, and Micayla runs back onto the stage.

"What was that all about?" I ask her.

"Nothing." She looks at me weirdly, like it's a bizarre question. I don't have time to say anything else, because Mr. Aprone tells us it's now round two.

"Name three of Sundae Best's retired flavors," he says.

Bennett whispers, "I got this one," and hits the buzzer. He answers, "Peach pistachio, caramel apple, and s'more explosion!"

"Yes!" Mr. Aprone matches Bennett's enthusiasm, and then everyone starts cheering. It's silly, but the fact that Bennett answered this question right immediately makes me feel better. Of course he knows the answer. He knows the Sundae Best flavors better than anyone.

But after that, things go downhill again. Sunny Days gets a question right about the consistency of sand, and No Sugar Added correctly answers a question about some old folksinger who performed on Seagate more than two hundred times. Then we get an answer right about the Seagate Book Club, since all our moms are in it.

But the final question is about the price of a summer home on Seagate in 1950, and we have absolutely no idea.

We lose.

The RemBenMic victory streak is over.

Bennett's leaving tomorrow for a four-day boat trip, and Micayla was whispering with Avery Sanders.

Maybe I'm being dramatic, but it feels like it's not just the Seagate Knowbodies contest that's over. It feels like Seagate life as I know it, and have always known it, is over too.

At least I have the dogs. That's what I keep telling myself. When everything else feels out of control, the dogs are reliable. In a way, dogs are better than people. They don't take their bad moods out on you, if they even get in bad moods. They don't let you down, and they're always pretty much the same.

Bennett plans to leave at ten in the morning. He told us last night to meet him at Mornings at nine. When I asked him why, he replied, "I want to say good-bye, duh," in this weird voice that made me wonder if he was kidding.

Micayla picks me up on the way, but she's not her usual cheery, morning-person self. Instead she's dragging her feet and rubbing her eyes and complaining.

"I want a day off from dog-sitting," she grumbles.

"Well, we got the morning off," I remind her. "So we could go meet Bennett for who knows what reason."

"Rem, he just wanted to say good-bye," she says, sounding exasperated. "You're overthinking it as usual."

After that, I stay quiet. It seems like I'm always saying the wrong thing, and it feels so bad that it makes me want to say nothing at all.

We get to Mornings, and Bennett is at the table with three chocolate croissants and three fresh-squeezed orange juices.

I get excited that it's just the three of us about to eat this amazingly yummy breakfast—but when I see Calvin come out of the bathroom, I feel out of sorts again.

"No croissant for you, Cal?" I ask.

"Cal?" Micayla says, and everyone laughs like it's totally strange that I called him that. It's just a nickname. Sheesh.

"I already had one," he says. Then there's an awkward silence, and I take a bite of mine just to have something to do.

Calvin's phone pings. He looks down and then says, "My dad wants us to meet at the main dock in twenty minutes. He got here early."

So Bennett shoves the whole croissant into his mouth and chugs his fresh-squeezed orange juice and burps as loud as I've ever heard anyone burp. No joke.

"Sorry to run out," he says, "but I have to go pick up my bag first."

"Yeah, and my dad gets really annoyed when people are late," Calvin tells us.

"Bye," I say quickly, not looking at either of them. "Have fun."

"Yeah, enjoy your bromance," Micayla teases, and I start laughing along with her.

"Ha-ha." Bennett gets up from the table and throws away his trash, and just like that he's off with Calvin, leaving Seagate, and us, behind.

"So we should probably go get the dogs, right?" Micayla asks me, looking down at her phone.

"Yeah," I reply.

We walk to Oscar's first and then to Marilyn Monroe's. Atticus and Rascal will meet us there. I wonder if we'll be okay handling two dogs each without Bennett to help with Frisbee and treats.

I count off how many days Bennett will be gone.

I've always missed him and been excited to see him, but this is different. This feels like a tiny part of my world is missing, like things won't be normal again until he's back. And the thing is, he was acting like a total doofus at the Seagate Knowbodies competition and even this morning, with the burping and running out like we didn't matter at all.

He wasn't acting like the Bennett I know. But I miss him anyway.

Rascal, Atticus, and Oscar are involved in a fierce game of chase-each-other-around-the-beach, and Micayla and I are sitting on the bench with Marilyn Monroe at our feet. We haven't said much to each other since breakfast, and I'm not sure why. Probably because I'm sad about Bennett leaving, but I think it could be more than that.

Micayla didn't really put much into the Seagate Knowbodies competition either, and after it was over, she seemed more relieved than anything else.

"Are you okay, Mic?" I have to ask. She's not herself, and

waiting around for someone to go back to being herself never works for me. I'm too impatient.

"Yeah. Fine. Why?" She looks down at the sand and not at me.

I continue to pet Marilyn Monroe, who is so happy to just be sitting between Micayla and me on this bench. She has no interest in being with the other dogs today. Maybe she could sense that we'd be feeling a little lonely without Bennett.

"You just don't seem like yourself," I say, because it's true.

"I'm fine, I said." She looks at me finally. "You're not acting like yourself either. I'm going to talk to Mason."

She gets up from the bench before I have a chance to say anything else and leaves me alone with Marilyn Monroe.

"Do you notice anything strange about her?" I ask Marilyn Monroe. She looks up at me and lets out a little whimper, then lies back down so I can rub her head.

I know that whimper. It means she agrees with me.

Across the beach I see Micayla talking to Mason Redmond. That's one thing that's changed. She doesn't run away from him anymore. Now she stands there, waving her arms, laughing. I wonder what they're talking about.

So I sit there on the bench and continue to feel sorry for myself. Marilyn Monroe doesn't mind it, and every few minutes I'll tell her how I'm feeling, and she'll whimper and look up at me, and it really makes me feel like she understands.

She's not Danish, but I never imagined I'd feel this close to a new dog so soon. Dogs can't be replaced. I think everyone knows that. But I'm realizing that it's possible to find an empty spot in your heart for a new one.

At the end of the day, Micayla and I round up Marilyn Monroe, Atticus, Oscar, and Rascal. We also offered to bring Palm home, because his owners were going for an early dinner at Picnic. We'll just let him in through the doggie door. They left food out for him and everything.

So Micayla walks with Oscar, Marilyn Monroe, and Atticus, and I have Palm and Rascal. The dogs are being good and not trying to run away or go off leash, but I can't wait to get them home and be done for the day. I'm feeling anxious about what's going on with Micayla. I don't know what it is, but things just don't seem quite right.

"So what are you doing tonight?" I ask Micayla after we drop off Oscar and Atticus.

"Hanging out with Avery," she says like it's no big deal. But they never hang out one-on-one.

"Really?" I ask.

"Yeah, really." Micayla crinkles her cheeks at me. "What's the big deal? She's our friend. And anyway, she's really fun this summer. You never even gave her a chance."

"That's not true." I smile, trying to make it seem like she's wrong and I don't care that she just said that. "Well. Have fun doing whatever you're doing."

"She's taking me on a tour of Seagate Schoolhouse."

"Um, okay," I reply, not knowing what to say to that. I didn't even know the schoolhouse was open during the summer.

"I'm becoming a year-rounder, Remy," Micayla says so quickly that I almost miss it.

"Oh." I'm so surprised, I lose my grip on the leashes I'm carrying, and the dogs start to run away. Thankfully, I get them back before they've gone too far.

Dogs, just behave right now. Please. I just got some huge news, and I can't focus on so much at once.

"I can't believe it," I say. "Did you just find out?"

"I'll explain after we've dropped off the dogs," she says, like she doesn't really want to talk about it but she's being forced to.

How could she have waited to tell me something so big?

We don't stay and chat with the dogs' owners as long as we usually do, and I feel a little bit bad about that. But when your best friend tells you huge news, you just don't have room for any other conversations.

After all the dogs are returned to their homes, we sit down on the Adirondack chairs by the stadium so we can talk without any interruptions.

"So did you just find out?" I ask again, looking down at my feet. My hot pink toenail polish is now chipped and baby pink from being exposed to so much sun.

"No." She doesn't look at me. "I've known since the end of the school year."

I nod and finally look up at her, and she's all slumped over her knees in the chair, instead of sitting back comfortably—the whole purpose of an Adirondack chair.

We sit there quietly, not talking, even though I have a million questions. Then I ask, "How come you didn't tell me?"

"Remy, you were so depressed about Danish, and then so busy with the dogs, and basically, I just didn't feel like you'd care that much." She finally leans back in the chair.

"Not care? Hello? Micayla, you're my best friend, and Seagate is my favorite place in the universe. How could I not care?" I feel myself yelling, and I don't want to yell. I don't want to be mad. I just can't understand this at all.

She's been keeping this from me for weeks. She's never kept a secret like this before—not that I know about, at least.

"I just wanted to enjoy the summer like we've always done," she tells me. "If you knew from the beginning, you'd be obsessing about it, telling me about which places stay open all year, who I should be friends with, y'know."

It's getting chilly, and I wish I had my hooded sweatshirt with me. I fold my arms across my chest to stay warm. "Well, I guess you don't want my opinions," I say. "Fine. Now I know."

"How about not thinking about yourself for one minute?" Micayla asks. "Okay? I'm telling you something big, and you're just focusing on how it affects you."

"I'm focusing on how I could have helped you. That's what friends do." I don't know what else to say, but words keep coming out of my mouth. "And I don't know why you're even stepping into a school in the summer. Summer is the one time when you can put school totally out of your head." Clearly,

I'm not only thinking about myself. I'm thinking about how I could've been a much better friend if I'd only known.

"Thanks for being so supportive," Micayala says, getting up from the chair. "I have to pick up a loaf of bread for my mom on the way home, so I'll just see you soon."

Micayla leaves me sitting there. I take the back way home, through the neighborhood, not on the main road. I don't want to see anyone. My hope is that stopping by my favorite house with the colored beach pails will cheer me up, but it doesn't.

Bennett's away, Micayla's mad at me, and all the dogs are at home for the night.

It feels like the time I got separated from my parents at the Museum of Modern Art. It only lasted a few minutes, but they were a dreadful few minutes. I was completely lost. I feel like that now. Lost and totally alone.

23

Later that evening, I decide to sit on the back porch and try to clear my thoughts. Our backyard has a perfect view of the ocean. I could sit out here for hours and hours doing nothing but staring at the sea. But I usually don't do that, because I'm always so busy.

I bring a book in case I need a break from sea gazing, but I don't get very far. I read a few words and then my mind wanders, and I can't seem to get it to pay attention to the book again. I don't know where things went wrong with Micayla. Maybe I should have responded differently, but I don't know what I should have said. Maybe if Bennett were home, he'd be able to help me make sense of things. I wonder if he knows already, and if he's been keeping it from me too.

Just as I'm about to ask my mom what's for dinner, I get a text from Claire:

Just my mom and me tonight. Going to F's Fish. Want 2 come?

On the one hand, it's surprising (and a little exciting) that Claire invited me to do something with her. I always thought she hated me. And maybe it will be good to get out and get my mind off things. On the other hand, it's Claire, and I'm never sure how she's going to act. She can invite me to dinner and be all nice about it and then act totally mean when I get there. But her mom's coming. And most people aren't mean in front of their moms.

I go inside and ask my parents if I can go, and then I remember that my dad had to go back to the city for a few days. That'll leave my mom home all alone for dinner, and I get lonely just thinking about it.

Well, if Claire's going with her mom, I can always ask if I can bring my mom along too. That's not weird, I don't think. Or maybe it is. But on Seagate, weird things are considered acceptable, sometimes even quirky and fun.

Can my mom come too? I text back.

A few seconds later, I get *TOTES* back from Claire and feel better already. Sometimes when you're feeling really down, a little invitation to do something makes everything feel better.

Claire kind of scares me. But right now going out to dinner with her and our moms feels like a scoop of ice cream on the hottest day of the summer.

"So you and Claire are friends now?" my mom asks me

as we're walking over to Frederick's Fish.

"I guess." I've been kicking a pebble down the path since we left our house, and I can tell it's driving my mom crazy. But I've gotten it so far, I can't stop now.

"You seem awfully quiet, Rem." She says it like a question, and I know she wants me to tell her what's on my mind. It's kind of strange how people use the word *awfully* to just mean *very* or *extremely*. That never really made sense to me.

I just shrug and don't really say anything. I'm upset about my conversation with Micayla, but I don't know how to tell my mom about it. Partly because I don't know if I'm right or Micayla's right. Maybe I *was* thinking about myself too much. But it wasn't like I did it to be mean. She didn't tell me what was going on.

We'll be at Frederick's Fish soon, and I'm sure Claire will talk about her jeans the whole time and save me from having to say much of anything at all. That's a good thing about someone like Claire—she'll talk and talk and talk, and you can just stay quiet if you want to.

I think I like being the quiet one. It's easier to listen to someone else than to talk about myself.

We get to Frederick's Fish, and Claire and her mom are sitting on the bench out front.

"Hello, I'm Iris, Claire's mom. Nice to meet you."

"I'm Abby," my mom replies.

They talk for a few minutes about Seagate life and remark on how odd it is that they don't remember each other as young girls spending summers on Seagate. I don't understand that at all. I know I'll remember everyone on Seagate when I'm my mom's age. I'll remember Mason Redmond and Avery Sanders and even people I'm not really friends with.

"Do you miss your brother?" I ask Claire, because I can't think of anything else to say.

"Not at all." She takes a lip gloss out of her cross-body bag and smears some on her lips. "He's gross. I wish I had a girl twin. Or a plain old sister."

"At least you have a sibling." I pick up the pebble that I kicked all the way here and put it in my pocket. It's so childish and superstitious, but something about that pebble feels lucky to me.

"You're not suffering that much, Remy." She rolls her eyes. That's the Claire I'm used to, but it doesn't seem to bother me as much today. She's being honest.

After a few minutes of awkward silence, Claire asks, "Where's Micayla tonight anyway? I was going to invite her too, but my mom said I could only invite one friend."

"Touring the school here." I force myself to say it without any commentary. I'll let Claire form her own opinion. Truth is, I wonder if Claire already knows about Micayla becoming a year-rounder. Maybe I was the last to find out. That might make me feel even worse than I do now.

"School?" Claire scoffs. "In July?"

I nod.

"That is just depressing."

"I agree! Thank you!" I'm immediately guilty for how excited I am about gossiping about Micayla. This isn't right. I know I'm doing the wrong thing, and yet I'm doing it anyway.

Luckily, the hostess at Frederick's Fish tells us that our table is ready, and she walks us to the back deck of the restaurant.

"Outside okay?"

"Of course!" my mom says. "The best view on Seagate!"

The hostess smiles and leaves us our menus. I'm not sure I agree about the view—there's the view from high up on the stage that's pretty awesome, and of course the one from the tippity-top of the lighthouse. But there are so many good views, it's hard to pick the best one.

"Where's Micayla tonight?" my mom asks me after we order our appetizers and our meals. So I explain the whole thing all over again.

"I see," my mom replies. She doesn't seem that surprised. Maybe she already knows. She probably does. She's pretty close with Micayla's mom.

Another person who knew before me.

"We're not attached at the hip, you know."

"Yeah you are," Claire says.

The waitress brings over a plate of fried zucchini sticks and a vegetable platter.

After she dips a zucchini stick into Frederick's secret sauce, Claire's mom says, "I was a year-rounder once." Which makes it sound like Claire already does know, or at least her mom already knows. Or maybe she's just bringing it up to make conversation.

"You were?" I ask.

Claire doesn't say anything, so I guess she already knows this story.

"For a year. My mom thought we needed a break from city life. My dad was depressed about the whole movie career bust, even though it had happened years and years before. We just sort of stepped out of regular society for a little while." She dips another zucchini stick. "And it was great. It was a chance to really spend time together and slow down our pace."

I nod. I wonder if she'd want to do that now, if she'd want to move here with Calvin and Claire for a year.

"It's not so bad, is all I'm saying." She smiles.

"Mom. Please don't tell me this is your way of breaking the news to me. I have Phoebe and Jenna at home. I can't just leave my best friends behind."

I wonder what "Home Claire" is like. I imagine her all popular, always invited to everything, the kind of girl other girls secretly hate but desperately want to be friends with at the same time.

Here on Seagate, it almost seems like she might like me. But at home, she probably wouldn't talk to me at all.

"Well, I don't know if Grandpa would be pleased with all of us just descending on his home for an entire year," Claire's mom says. "But it's something to think about. I hate that there's so much pressure on you in Westchester."

"I hate that too," my mom admits. "It's so tough, but I have come to accept that there is no perfect place to live."

The moms go on and on about this—suburbs versus the city, living on Seagate year-round, all of that. Claire and I stare at each other for a few seconds before she starts to tell me this story about her friends Jenna and Phoebe and how they got in trouble for skipping band last year.

"So what was the punishment?" I ask.

"We had to go five minutes late to lunch," Claire says. "I was totally freaked out that we wouldn't get our usual table, but we did. And there wasn't even a long line for food by the time we got there. So it ended up being not that bad."

"That's good," I say. My stomach grumbles so loudly that Claire and I both start cracking up.

"What are you like at home?" Claire asks. "Are you, like, friends with everybody? Just a small group? Or what?"

I dip a zucchini stick, partly because I'm hungry and partly because I want the time to think of the right answer. She wants to know if I'm popular.

"I don't know what I am. I guess I'm somewhere in the middle."

Thankfully, Claire doesn't press it further. I want to tell her I liked it better when we never used to think about these things. We were just ourselves, and that was good enough. But maybe she knows that. Maybe she didn't used to think about these things either.

Our fish sandwiches come, and we dig into the delicious-ness that is Frederick's Fish. Nothing else really matters when you're eating a Frederick's Fish Sandwich. It's pretty much perfection in a sandwich.

After dinner, we all walk home together, and we find Mr. Brookfield sitting on the front porch. "Hope you ladies enjoyed dinner," he says. "We played three games of canasta, and my team won every time."

We all congratulate him and his teammate Mr. Mayer, from around the corner.

"And I heard from the boys," Mr. Brookfield tells us. "They're having a blast."

I'm glad that Bennett's having fun, but I also hate it. I hate that he's having a blast without me, without Seagate. What if he comes home and he's better friends with Calvin than he'll ever be with me again?

I never used to think about these things. Like popularity, they never used to matter. But they matter now, and as much as I tell myself that they don't and that things are exactly the same, I know it's not true.

24

*It seems like a million dogs have descended on Sea-*gate—right when Bennett is away and Micayla and I are fighting. Micayla and I still see each other, but she hasn't asked me to go swimming or go to Sundae Best since our fight. When we're with the dogs, she hangs out more with them than with me, and we haven't said more than five words to each other in the last few days.

One morning I get a call from a woman named Betty. She's an artist and she was just commissioned to paint a mural in one of the biggest houses on Seagate. She'll be gone for most of the day, and she's heartbroken about leaving her beagle, Tabby, home by herself. Of course I agreed to take on another dog, and I'm happy to do it.

But that isn't the only call I get. We also need to look after a collie named Potato Salad (and I thought Marilyn Monroe was a weird name for a dog!) for a few hours this week while his owner goes for physical therapy off-island. And then there's a new family with a cocker spaniel, Lester. The only thing is, the house they're renting doesn't really allow dogs, so they're trying to keep him outside as much as possible.

That brings the dog tally to seven: Oscar, Rascal, Atticus, Marilyn Monroe, Tabby, Potato Salad, and Lester. And only Micayla and me around to work.

I sit at the kitchen table and make a list of all the dogs and their needs, carefully writing down who needs to be picked up and returned and who will be dropped off. Thankfully, Bennett will be coming back in two days. I hope he'll be excited to hear about the new dogs, and happy to see me too.

I'm all ready to go get Oscar and Atticus for the morning shift when my phone rings. It's Micayla. Strange that she's calling instead of just coming over.

"Hi, Mic," I say, as cheerful as can be, hoping if I'm friendly, we can just pretend we never had a fight at all.

"Don't kill me, Remy. Okay?"

When people say *Don't kill me*, they're pretty much warning you that they're about to say or do something really annoying and you should be ready. Also, they're saying that they know they're doing something wrong, but they're going to do it anyway, and you just have to accept it.

"What?"

I can hear her taking a deep breath through the phone. "I need a day off."

I know she's talking about the doggie day care business, but it occurs to me that maybe she means a day off from our friendship. I'm mad and worried at the same time.

"Why?"

"You're going to think this is lame, but Avery Sanders just found out that there's another new girl on Seagate. She just moved here, and she's going to be a year-rounder too. And I feel like I should meet her so I know another new person."

I want to be understanding. I want to say that it's totally fine and that I would want to do the same thing if I were her. I know Micayla has to do this. But it still hurts. It still feels like I am being left behind.

Maybe it wasn't just that she waited so long to tell me. Maybe I also feel like I'm being replaced by Avery Sanders.

"Fine. Whatever. I have to get the dogs." I wait for her to say something else, but she doesn't. I don't know if I should tell her about our three new clients. I doubt she'd even care.

"I'll call you later," Micayla says.

"Don't bother. You're obviously not carrying your weight in this business. You have other things to focus on right now. Go hang out with Avery Sanders and the new girl." I end the call and feel even worse than I did yesterday.

Bennett's away, and he has a new BFF anyway. Micayla's moving on and staying in the same place at the same time. And I'm just here, same as I ever was. Things are changing all around me, and I can't do anything about it.

But I don't have time to think about any of it now. I'm late to get Oscar and Atticus, and I have to be at Dog Beach in twenty minutes to meet the others. I hate being late!

When I get to my first stop, Dawn is already waiting outside with Oscar. He's running in circles on the lawn as Dawn holds one baby over her shoulder and the other two whimper in their stroller. I quickly attach Oscar's leash and run to get Atticus. Paul is waiting outside too, and Atticus is sitting next to him. I get the sense that Paul wants to chat, but there's no time for that now. I can't be late for the others.

I run and try to get to the beach before any of the other dogs. But Lester is already there waiting with his family.

"We needed him out of the house bright and early," the dad says. "The owners of the house apparently live on Seagate too! We're totally going to get busted."

He doesn't seem nervous, so I laugh, thinking that he's making some kind of joke. Lester joins Oscar and Atticus and they all start playing, and soon after, Marilyn Monroe arrives unexpectedly.

Amber goes on and on about how Hudson used to sleep through the night and now he's not, and she really needs a babysitter so she can find time to work out. She's always stressed about something, and I just don't have the time or energy to deal with it today.

"I guess you don't have time for more babysitting with all your dog-sitting, Remy," she says. "Any other suggestions?"

"I don't know. I'll think about it," I tell her. I hate to be short with her, but this woman basically needs me to be her full-time child and dog nanny, and I can't. I have enough problems of my own.

When it's just Oscar, Atticus, Lester, and Marilyn Monroe, everything feels easy and smooth. But then Rascal arrives, and he's all out of sorts today—rambunctious, barking, tormenting the other dogs. It's so unlike him. I wonder if he woke up on the wrong side of the crate. Even his velvety fur doesn't look as smooth today.

In a way, he's acting how I feel—totally out of control. And the more I try to control him, the crazier he gets. Maybe dogs are kind of like people and they don't like to be told what to do or bossed around.

I try to introduce all the regular dogs to the newcomers, but almost all of them seem a little shy and not so eager to make new friends. Except for Lester. He runs around, paying attention to all the other dogs. In a way, he feels like my assistant today in trying to keep everyone happy. Maybe I should just keep him with me for the rest of the time his family is here.

I keep encouraging all the dogs to play together, but they just turn away and go back to the dogs that they know. They seem as resistant to change as I am, and from the outside, it's frustrating.

"You're here alone today?" Mason Redmond asks. I didn't even see him walking over. I notice he's wearing a whistle, and I wonder if it's at all effective when the dogs swim out too far.

"Yeah. Unfortunately." Rascal comes over for a treat, and then Potato Salad wants one, and soon all the dogs are at my feet waiting for their morning snack.

"You're handling it pretty well." He gives me two thumbs up, and I notice his nails are dirty. It's pretty gross. A "forward thinker" should have clean nails.

"Thanks." Tabby's the last to get a treat, and she licks my arm after she gets it. I think that's her way of saying thank you. Her ears flop back and forth as she runs toward the ocean. Beagles are such happy-go-lucky dogs—I wish I could borrow her attitude. "We'll see."

"Well, if you need any help, I'll be over there on the old lifeguard's chair." He points to the tall wooden chair a few feet away from the water. Usually it cracks me up that he sits there for most of the day, just watching, not really interacting with the dogs. He's more of a dog lifeguard than a volunteer at Dog Beach. But today it only makes me sad. Everything is bothering me, and this is just one more thing to add to the list.

"Thanks, Mason."

"And you'll probably be really hungry when this day's over, after working so hard and everything." He pauses and starts twirling the string of his whistle around his fingers, the way real lifeguards always do. "So if you want to go to Sundae Best, I'll totally go with you. I think today's the day they're unveiling their latest signature flavor."

"Oh, I think it's mango something," I start to say, and then

I get a funny feeling. Mason Redmond is asking me to go to Sundae Best with him. Just the two of us?

"Yeah, I heard mango too, but that could be a rumor." He turns around when he notices one of the dogs is too far out. He blows his whistle and motions for the dog to come back, but I'm not even sure the dog can see or hear him, and I'm certain the dog's owner is here somewhere watching anyway.

"I'd better run," he says. "But let me know if you, um, want to go. We can discuss the dogs, and ideas for the business and stuff."

Mason sprints across the sand, tripping a few times and losing a flip-flop along the way. I wonder what Micayla sees in him. Still, it was nice of him to ask me and offer ideas for the business. On a day when I was feeling like the biggest loser in the world, it was nice for someone, even Mason Redmond, to ask me to go to Sundae Best with him.

The day goes downhill after that. Potato Salad gets completely tangled in seaweed, and it takes three people (me, Mason, and a stranger) to untangle her. Then Atticus seems to have a stomachache, because he poops about five times and it's very difficult to clean up. And Marilyn Monroe just wants to sit by my side and be petted. She keeps putting her paw on my leg and then barking when I don't go back to petting her.

Luckily, Rascal's mood has improved and he seems to be bonding with Lester. Oscar is happy because he found a kid to play Frisbee with.

But when it's time to take everyone home, all the leashes get tangled up with one another, and it takes me fifteen minutes to untangle them.

Everything is totally out of control. Micayla bailed on me, Bennett is away, and now even the dogs are going nuts. Dog-sitting was supposed to be fun and low-key, not super stressful. And I was supposed to be doing it with my friends, not all alone.

And just as I'm walking out of Dog Beach, I see Micayla walking with Avery Sanders and the mysterious new year-rounder girl. The new girl has those fancy jean shorts on. I only recognize them because Claire has a pair.

"So no Sundae Best with me?" Mason yells as I'm halfway out the gate. I totally forgot about his offer, but it would have been too weird to go anyway, especially dragging along seven dogs.

"Sorry." I shrug. "Next time. Okay?"

He nods reluctantly and blows his whistle for the millionth time.

I'm finally out the gate and onto the pavement with all seven dogs following behind me, and there's Micayla, standing right in front of me.

"You and Mason? Sundae Best?"

"Don't even ask," I mumble.

"I won't. You know I like him, Remy." She turns away, walking again with Avery and fancy-shorts year-rounder girl.

It takes me the whole walk to Oscar's house to understand what just happened. Micayla thinks I like Mason now. She thinks I tried to get him to ask me to go to Sundae Best. No way. No way at all.

I'll have to explain. I have to make her listen.

I may have said some mean things the past few days, but I'd never steal her crush. That's against all the best-friend codes of conduct in the world. I may only be eleven, but even I know that.

When all the dogs are returned to their homes, I decide to go for a walk. Alone. It's rare that I want to be alone on Seagate, but I'm exhausted from such a busy day taking care of the dogs, and I need to figure out what to say to Micayla. I want to make it right and explain what happened with Mason, but I'm also still upset that she kept a secret from me. I'm not the only one who needs to apologize.

I text my mom to tell her I'm going for a walk, so she won't worry. I walk to the beach and then across the boardwalk, down the path to the main part of Seagate, past Sundae Best—there's a line all the way down the street waiting for the unveiling of its new flavor—and I keep walking, past Picnic and Mornings and the Dollhouse Café, past Novel Ideas Book Shop and Frederick's Fish and the art gallery. I walk the whole perimeter of the island. I see Bennett's mom picking Asher up from day camp, but I look away before she sees me. I don't want to say hi to anyone, because I'd have to pretend I was fine and I'm not. I keep walking, not even stopping to see who's playing Ping-Pong.

Finally I decide to sit down on one of the benches at the far end of the island, near the lighthouse. I look under the bench to see if any of our chalk drawings from last summer are still there. I know they're gone, but I look anyway, just to see if maybe the tiniest bit of chalk didn't get washed away by rain.

I wish I could be one of those people who can roll with the punches, who jumps into any new situation with open arms and an open mind. That's Bennett. Nothing fazes him. He can be thrown into a roomful of strangers and be totally fine. His mom could tell him tomorrow that they were becoming year-rounders, and he wouldn't even stress about it. He'd find a year-rounder friend and play Ping-Pong and be as happy as can be.

I'm the opposite, and I hate that about myself.

But maybe I just need to accept myself and how I react. And maybe I just need to accept the chaos and not try too hard to tame it. Maybe I just need to accept my weird feelings about Bennett, and that Micayla is making new friends. Maybe worrying is just making the problems seem bigger and making me feel worse.

I see Mr. Brookfield walking toward me out of the corner of my eye, and I try to look away, look down at my feet or gaze at the ocean, so he doesn't see me. I like him, but I just don't feel like talking to him right now.

"Funny meeting you here," he says.

I guess there was no way of avoiding saying hi.

"Hi."

"I thought this was my bench," he says, sitting down. "Usually I'm all alone when I come here."

"I was alone until you got here."

"A penny for your thoughts, Remy," he says. He even hands me a penny, and I hold it in my hand, planning to save it for later when I'll throw it into the wishing well.

"Well, I gave you the penny," he reminds me after we're quiet for a few seconds. "So start talking."

"I don't know what to say," I admit. "I'm just feeling a little blue."

"Still about that dog of yours?"

It takes me a minute to understand what he's talking about. Of course—he's thinking of Danish. It surprises me, because I actually haven't missed Danish as much lately.

"No." I shake my head. "Just a really tiring day." I tell him how I'm so tired from watching the dogs today and how it was hard to do it alone, and I tell him about the whole tangled seaweed incident and the other stuff. I explain that the more I try to control the dogs' behavior, the crazier they act.

He half smiles. "I think there's more going on inside that head of yours."

"I guess it's everything, really." I shrug.

He folds his arms behind his head. "Go on."

I don't know if I even want to unload all of this right now, but I guess it's better than keeping it locked up in my thoughts.

"Well, everything feels so different than it was last summer and all the summers before. My friends don't want to do the same things we always did before. And I guess I just don't know what to do. I don't know how to make things go back to the way they used to be." I can't look at him. I can't look at anyone right now. Eye contact with another human would only make me start to cry. A dog would be okay, maybe. But a human, no.

"Things don't always go back to the way they used to be," Mr. Brookfield says. His legs are stretched out in front of him, and his tube socks are pulled up to his knees. At least the way he dresses always stays the same. "Believe me. I know that personally."

I hand him the penny. "Now your turn."

He chuckles a little. "I spent years wishing things could go back to the way they were when I was in the movies, when I was auditioning, when my scream was a big deal." He sighs, and I worry that he'll start to cry. "And the years I spent wishing that things would be back to the way they used to be were years that I wasted. Years that I didn't pay as much attention to my children and my wife, years that I didn't pursue new hobbies and learn new things."

I swallow hard. I'm a different kind of sad now—sad for him and not for me.

"And I still long for the old days, believe me. The old days of the movies, sure. But other old days—when my children were young." He smiles and hands the penny back to me.

"But the new days are good days too. And if we spend too long thinking about how to get the old days back, we miss the new days. The new days are the important ones."

I nod. "But what do you do when the new days seem so strange? And everything changes so fast, before you even have time to prepare for it or to see it coming?"

"It's hard," he says. "I'm not going to tell you that it's easy."

"But you'll tell me that everything will be okay?" I look at him, finally. He has bright blue eyes, and I never noticed. I guess that's where Calvin and Claire get their blue eyes.

He readjusts a tube sock, and I wonder if this is a good time to suggest sandals. Wearing sneakers and socks on Seagate is practically a crime. "I promise you that everything will be okay . . . eventually," he says. "And things will be okay before you even realize that they're okay. So make sure you pay attention."

"I'll try to believe you."

He looks at his watch. "It's almost six! And it's pizza night in the Brookfield home. You're coming, right?"

"I wouldn't miss it."

"Too bad the boys are coming back tomorrow," Claire says, putting on the Scream recording. I'm surprised that she does that, because Bennett's always the one to put it on, and Claire's always the one to complain about it. "It's been so quiet and un-gross without them. Right?"

"I guess." *Un-gross* is a funny way to describe it. I grab a mushroom slice from the box. "Maybe it's been too quiet?"

"Well, it's just you and me tonight. I texted Micayla to come, but she asked if you were coming, and when I said yes, she said she was busy." Claire narrows her eyes at me. "What's that all about?"

I take my slice and a glass of lemonade to the green Adirondack chair and hope I can find a way to change the topic.

"Come on, what's going on with you guys?" Claire asks, sitting in the blue Adirondack chair next to me. "I thought you guys didn't fight all the time. I thought you were different from Phoebe, Jenna, and me."

"I thought so too."

"So?" she asks.

"So, I don't know." It comes out more harshly than I'd meant it to.

"Okay. Sheesh."

I sit farther back in my chair and we eat our pizza quietly. Even though Claire has grown on me, I wish these weekly pizza dates hadn't become a tradition. Mr. Brookfield thinks I'm some kind of crazy person now, and Claire thinks I'm a mean friend.

I keep counting the minutes until Bennett gets back, but even when he does, it's not like I can expect him to make everything better all on his own.

"Do you think Micayla has a crush on my brother?" Claire asks, totally out of the blue. Maybe she was tired of the silence. Or maybe she really has been wondering.

"What?" I ask, not able to hide my shock. "Um, no."

"Hey! Don't say it like that."

"Say it like what?" I turn to look at her and notice she has some pizza sauce in the corner of her mouth. "You said yourself he's gross."

"I'm allowed to say it." She glares at me. "He's my brother. You're not allowed to say it."

"Okay." I'm confused but don't want to admit it. "I'm sorry."

Claire gets up to grab another slice. When she comes back, she asks, "So does she?"

"Honestly, I don't think so. She likes Mason Redmond." I sip my lemonade and debate saying anything more about how he invited me to Sundae Best and how Micayla thought I was interested in him. Maybe I shouldn't have even told Claire about the whole Micayla and Mason thing. Is this another thing she'll be mad at me for?

"Oh, Mason—the kid who helps at Dog Beach?" she asks.

I nod. "Yeah, I don't really get what she sees in him. He's kind of nerdy."

Claire cracks up. "Hello? Remy? You started a day camp for dogs. That's a little bit nerdy too."

I should probably shrug off her comment, but it stings. It seemed like Claire and I were finally becoming friends, and now she's making fun of me.

"Aw, don't go cry about it." She nudges me with her shoulder. "You want brownies? I made some earlier."

We go inside and have brownies, but I keep thinking about what she said. And I wonder about Micayla. Maybe she really does like Calvin but hasn't told me. She's kept other secrets. I want to know why Claire asked, but I feel too uncomfortable.

"You didn't need to say my business idea was nerdy." I finally get the courage to say it when we're up in Claire's room and she's going through her jean collection for the millionth time.

"I was kidding, Remy." She throws a T-shirt at me. It still

has the tags on, and it cost more than fifty dollars. "I still think you're cool, even with your nerdy business. Don't be so sensitive."

Claire thinks I'm cool. Really? I mean, I know she wouldn't say it unless she meant it. That's the thing about Claire. She says what she thinks—whether it's appropriate or not, whether it's nice or not. It's kind of helpful to have a friend like that.

A little while later, Claire and Mr. Brookfield offer to walk me home, but I tell them that I'm fine on my own.

The truth is, I just want some time to clear my head.

I thought I was feeling so much better after the talk with Mr. Brookfield and after that dinner with Claire and her mom, but I'm just as confused as ever. The dog-sitting business is going well, but Micayla and I are in our first real fight, and I have all these feelings about Bennett that I don't know what to do with.

It's like a mosquito bite that just keeps itching and itching. The more I scratch it, the worse it gets.

26

I can't fall asleep that night, so I text Micayla at eleven thirty. I wouldn't normally do that, but it's summer and people stay up late. And I'm not sure I can go another day being in this fight with Micayla. It's too painful.

Come to my house for breakfast tomorrow before dogs. We need to talk.

I wait and wait and wait for a response. Finally, an hour later, she writes.

Will let u know in AM

But when morning rolls around, I still haven't heard from her. I assume that she's coming and that she just forgot to text me back. I decide to scramble some eggs and toast some rye bread. I'll even cut up strawberries and bananas and put some grapefruit juice in a pitcher.

My mom comes in, frazzled because she's late for a meeting with the Seagate Community Association. "Ooh, maybe I'll take some fruit to go," she says. "Wait. Did you make this for me?"

I shake my head. "No. For Micayla. I hope she's coming."

"Is everything okay, Rem? I'm starting to worry."

"It's okay. Go to your meeting. You're going to be late."

She nods reluctantly and gives me a kiss on the cheek. "I'll see you this afternoon. You and I have a date. We're splitting a banana split. No arguing!"

"Deal." I smile. Then I start digging through the pots and pans for the little omelet pan. I can't make an omelet in any pan but this one.

I know it's a little bit weird to have so many feelings about an omelet pan, but there's a good reason for it. It's so small and perfect for making eggs for one or two people. On the other hand, I also hate it. I hate it because I imagine Grandma making eggs in it, all by herself. She never had people over for breakfast, so when she was using this pan, she was all alone. I hate to think about her all alone on Seagate during the year, without us. But then I get happy using this pan because it makes me think of Grandma, and I like thinking about her.

It's confusing how I can really think this much about a tiny frying pan.

I continue with the breakfast even though I'm not sure if Micayla is coming or not. Luckily, the doorbell rings at nine thirty, so all this food will not go to waste.

"Smells good," Micayla says, not really looking at me. She comes right in and takes a seat at the kitchen table. She pours herself a glass of grapefruit juice and butters her toast before I've even sat down.

I'm glad that she still feels comfortable here. Sure, it's only been a few days of awkwardness between us, but it feels much longer.

"I guess this is your way of apologizing?" Micayla asks me, after spooning some eggs onto her plate.

I pour myself some juice and try to figure out what to say. "Well, I just wanted to talk to you."

"Talk to me about how you're stealing Mason Redmond? And have become a totally mean friend?"

"Huh?"

"He asked you to go to Sundae Best. I heard it."

"I don't like him like that."

"Why? What's so bad about him that you don't like him?"

"Well, he only wanted to go to Sundae Best to discuss the dog-sitting business. That's what I mean. It wasn't, like, a date. If that's what you were thinking."

I take a small bite of eggs. I'm not really sure what's happening right now, but it's not the way I wanted the conversation to go. "But anyway, I wanted to talk to you about other stuff. I wasn't only thinking about the Mason thing."

"Of course you weren't," Micayla says. "You always think about yourself. That's the problem. When you were sad about Danish, I did everything to cheer you up. And when you wanted to do the doggie day care, I did everything I could to help. But now that I'm going to be a year-rounder on Seagate, you don't care. And even the whole Mason thing, you don't care about that either."

"Micayla, that's not true."

"It is true, Remy." She pushes her chair back from the table, and it makes a terrible screeching sound. "I have to give up all my friends and my whole life, and you don't even want to talk about it. For one second, think about somebody other than yourself."

Micayla walks out of my house without saying anything else. That wasn't at all how I expected this breakfast to go, and I don't have time to get upset about it. I have to clean up all the dishes and go get the dogs. But when I look at today's schedule, there's a huge problem. I am watching all of our usuals: Oscar, Atticus, Rascal, Marilyn Monroe, plus Tabby and Potato Salad. But I also said I could keep an eye on Palm and the pair of Malteses. That's nine dogs. And one me.

There's no way I can handle that.

And now that Micayla wants nothing to do with me, there's only one person I can call to help.

"Claire," I say as soon as she picks up the phone.

"Yeah," Claire answers.

"It's Remy."

"I know." She pauses. "What's up?"

I take a deep breath and pray that this works. I have ten minutes before I need to be at Oscar's. "I need your help. I know you said that the dog-sitting thing was nerdy. And I know you think I'm too sensitive. But I'm begging you. Can you please help me with the dogs today?"

"Really?" she asks, and I'm expecting her to tell me she's busy ironing her jeans again or she has to go to the pool and work on her tan.

"Yeah."

"I thought you'd never ask!"

"Huh?"

"Remy, I've been waiting for you to ask me to work with the dogs all summer. But I figured you didn't like me and didn't want me around, so I never asked."

"I had no idea," I admit.

"I'll meet you at Oscar's in five minutes," she tells me.

"You know where Oscar lives?"

"Yeah." I hear the creak of her closet door in the background. "I pay attention, Remy."

It turns out Claire is awesome with the dogs. Marilyn Monroe loves her instantly, and I swear they're sitting on the bench together talking about jeans. Even though Marilyn doesn't wear them, she seems like she'd be very into fashion. Marilyn Monroe barks and Claire turns around to show her the stitching on her jean shorts. It's very funny to watch. But it's not only Marilyn Monroe who Claire's great with—she's also great at rubbing Potato Salad's tummy in just the right spot, and Rascal has a good time splashing with her in the waves.

I wonder why I've waited so long to ask Claire to hang out with the dogs. And when I think about that, I start to feel bad. You really don't know what goes on inside someone's head until she chooses to tell you—or you choose to ask. I don't think I've been doing enough asking.

"We still need to go to Sundae Best together," Mason says, catching me totally off guard when I'm at the water fountain filling up the dogs' bowls. "I think I have more good ideas for your business. Whenever you have time."

"Okay, hopefully we will find some time."

I look over at Claire, who's playing Frisbee with Atticus and Rascal while Marilyn Monroe watches from a few feet away. She's throwing the Frisbee and chatting with Marilyn Monroe, and I swear I've never seen her happier. Not even when she's talking about her jeans.

Maybe I could borrow her honesty and say something important.

"Mason, I have to tell you something," I say.

"Yeah?" He perks up and then looks out into the ocean to make sure all the swimming dogs are okay.

"You should ask Micayla to go to Sundae Best."

"Huh?" He blows his whistle for no real reason, but I can tell he feels most comfortable when he's in charge.

"I mean, not just to discuss dog-sitting. I just think she'd like it if you asked her," I say. "I'm just telling you, because, um, in case you didn't know."

He nods. "Okay, Remy. I'd better get back to the lifeguard's chair. The water can be dangerous for these little guys." He pets Marilyn Monroe, who has just run over to us and is now sitting at Mason's feet. I pet her too. I wonder if she can see the difference in me—how honest and open I'm being.

At the end of the day, Claire and I walk the dogs home and I tell her how great she was. "Seriously, you're amazing with dogs."

"Thanks." She smiles. "They're awesome. I think I might want to be a dog groomer one day. But more like a dog stylist. Or maybe I could just come up with an upscale fashion line for dogs. Doggie Couture or something."

"All good ideas."

After all the dogs are dropped off, I ask her if she wants to come over for dinner. "I think it's taco night," I tell her. "My dad is back in the city, and my mom is really into tacos. She makes all kinds of fillings—fish, tofu, chicken, beef. She brings everything over to the table, and we can make our own combinations."

I feel silly getting so excited about taco night, but I can't help it.

"Sounds delish. I'll ask Grandpa," she says. "Oh wait, but Calvin and my dad are back. I'll probably have to see them. Boring."

"I understand." I hadn't thought about Bennett coming back for most of the day. Now I'm nervous all over again. I can't keep my feelings a secret anymore. I don't even know what the feelings are, but Claire inspired me today. You have to speak up. And when you do, amazing things can happen.

"You told Mason about Micayla, didn't you?" she asks. We're standing outside Mr. Brookfield's house, and part of me wants to run home but part of me wants to stay so that I can see Bennett.

"How did you know?"

"He asked me about it," she says. "He was like 'what do you know about Micayla Walcott?'"

"And?"

"And I said I didn't really know much, and then he said you told her that he should ask her to go to Sundae Best, and the whole thing was so funny to me that I just started cracking up."

"Why?" Now I'm laughing, though I'm not really sure why.

"He's just so weird!" Now we're both cracking up, not really about Mason and not really about Micayla. I'm not even sure what we're laughing about. But in the middle of the full-out laughing session, two things occur to me:

1. Claire and I are real friends now. Only real friends have this kind of cracking-up moment.
2. Bennett and Calvin are watching this whole thing.

"We're baaaaack," Calvin says. "Miss us?"

"Yeah, right." Claire looks at me. "On second thought, Remy, maybe I will come for those tacos. And then maybe I will move in with you too?"

"Tacos? Abby Boltuck's famous taco night?" Bennett asks, and my heart immediately feels warm and happy, the way it does after I've had a bowl of lobster bisque at Frederick's Fish.

Bennett remembers everything.

"Yup" is all I can manage to say. I want to invite him over, but there's too much that I have to say. I wouldn't be able to eat the tacos, and I can't do that to my mom. Our conversation will have to wait. At least until after taco night.

"So what were you guys laughing about?" Calvin asks, zooming me back into the conversation.

I look at Claire and Claire looks at me.

"Just girl stuff," she says.

It's been almost a week and Micayla's still not talking to me. Bennett stopped by her house the other day to say hi, and he said she was kind of cold to him too. We don't really know what to do about it. We've never seen her like this.

Thankfully, Claire loves helping with the dogs. And Calvin seems pretty into it too. He really only pays attention to Rascal, but it's okay. I think Rascal needs some one-on-one time.

"So. Two questions," Claire starts when we're on our way to Dog Beach. We've picked up Oscar, Marilyn Monroe, and Palm. The boys are getting the others.

"Yeah?" I ask, admiring the rhinestone bow Marilyn Monroe is wearing today. I've been searching online for doggie hair bows, so I can send her one for the holidays. I kind of want to make sure she remembers me during the rest of the year.

"When are you going to admit that you're in love with Bennett? And when are you going to make up with Micayla?"

That's another thing that's changed since Claire and I have become friends. She'll just ask really bold questions like it's no big deal at all. Basically, whatever's on her mind will come out of her mouth.

It took her pretty much all summer to say that she loved dogs and wanted to help out with the business. And now she'll say anything.

It's kind of crazy how someone can change so much in such a short amount of time. Or maybe Claire didn't really change—I was just willing to look at her in a different way.

Claire's personality is part awesome and part scary. I never know what she's going to say, and in a way I'm always worried that she'll embarrass me. But the good part is that she brings hard-to-talk-about things out into the open, and that can be really helpful.

"I guess my answer is the same for both questions," I reply. "I don't know."

"Oh." Claire looks at me, but I don't make eye contact with her. I feel exposed, like she just walked in on me changing out of a bathing suit. "I need to tell you one thing, though. About Micayla. You're being kind of selfish, you know. She's the one going through this whole big change. All you need to do is be understanding. So what if she didn't tell you right away? Maybe it was hard for her. Anyway, it's boring to talk about this, so that's all I'm going to say."

Her honesty stings the way it usually does, but maybe she's right. She probably is.

"Thanks. I'll think about it." I can't look at her. "But how did you know? About the Bennett thing, I mean. Did your grandfather tell you?" I look at her, finally.

"What? My grandfather?" She laughs. "Why would he know?"

"No reason." I guess she doesn't know about our conversation, and now I feel weird talking about it. But it's pretty clear that Mr. Brookfield isn't very gossipy. He kept his scream a secret for all these years.

"I know about your crush because it's crazy obvious," Claire says. "The way you act when he's around—all nervous but chatty. The way you look at him. They way you bring him up in conversations when we're not even talking about him at all."

"Oh." I look down at my feet, and at the dogs, basically anywhere but at Claire. I feel even more exposed now, like I'm walking to Dog Beach totally naked.

I wait for her to say something about Bennett. Maybe that he acts the same way around me. Or that she's overheard him talking to Calvin about me. Or anything, really. But she doesn't. The conversation ends there, and I'm not sure if we'll ever talk about it again. I'm not sure if I ever want to talk about it again.

The dogs are all thrilled to be at Dog Beach, and they're behaving themselves, so there's not much for me to do.

They're all playing happily. The boys are keeping some of them busy with a wild game of Frisbee. Potato Salad and Tabby are sunbathing together. They're the oldest dogs of the bunch and they love to lie around, but they love to lie around together. Whenever one's there without the other, they just roam around gloomily. Lester continues to be the social butterfly, spending a little time with each dog.

After all the dogs are settled, I decide to walk around the beach a little bit and check on them individually. I always focus on them as a group, but they're all a little like Rascal: They need their one-on-one time.

As I'm walking around, I notice that Mason Redmond isn't here. He's been here every single day this summer, and he never mentioned that he was going off-island or anything. I wonder if he's sick.

Claire and I are sitting on the bench mapping out a plan for the rest of the day. Most of the dog owners wanted a full day of care today, so we had to plan it all out. We collected bowls and plastic bags of food from all the owners this morning so everyone will have something to eat. Sometimes Tabby and Potato Salad like to nap after lunch, so they can just do that on the beach. Marilyn Monroe spends most of the day lounging anyway, and she's happy to be outside.

When it comes to Rascal, Atticus, and Oscar, they're happy as long as they're playing and they're fed. Lester just likes to keep busy. And Palm is being picked up at noon, so we didn't need to worry about his lunch.

"Ooh, your boyfriend is coming over." I look up, expecting to see Mason, since Claire likes to make fun of the whole "let's go to Sundae Best together" thing, even though he only wanted to discuss the dogs. But it's Bennett walking over to us. I hope he didn't hear her say that.

"Weird that Mason's not here, right?" He looks at me. It's like he just read my mind. "Is it safe for the dogs to be swimming unsupervised?" He laughs and I do too, and then I feel bad for making fun of Mason. It's true that he's not really a dog lifeguard, but he takes his pretend job seriously.

"Maybe he's sick," I say.

"Sickly in love with Remy!" Calvin yells, and then Bennett and Calvin high-five. Claire gives them a "come on" kind of look, and my face feels like it's resting on a campfire.

"Maybe that's why Micayla's so mad at you," Bennett says. "You stole her man."

"Ugh, my man? Seriously? And I didn't steal anyone." I don't know how I manage to get the words out, but I do. "I need to go fill up Atticus's water bowl. He looks parched."

I get up and walk away, but I hear them whispering behind me. I plan to take a very long time filling up Atticus's bowl. I should have brought all the dogs' bowls over and filled each of them one by one.

As I'm walking back, trying carefully not to spill all the water, I see Claire running over to me. Immediately I assume something is wrong with one of the dogs, and my heart starts pounding. Maybe we took on too many clients. Maybe we weren't ready. Maybe Calvin doesn't take this seriously enough.

"What's wrong?" I ask.

"You're going to kill me."

"What did you do to Marilyn Monroe's hair?" I ask. Claire has been threatening to style it in some wacky way, and I have forbidden her to do it.

"It's not that," she says tentatively. "It's worse."

"What did you do?" I ask, even though I already know the answer. I see Bennett and Calvin out of the corner of my eye. Marilyn Monroe is sitting all alone on the bench, and I need to go over there but I'm scared to.

"I'm sorry. It's just they were saying that you loved Mason or that Mason loved you and it was so untrue, and I knew you were never going to admit your feelings to Bennett and I couldn't help myself. So *I* had to." She's digging a hole in the sand with the toe of her sparkly flip-flop, and all I want right now is for that hole to be big enough for me to fit inside it.

"What do I do now?" I ask. I don't know if I will ever be able to talk to Bennett again. The secret is out and things will never go back to normal. I'm too afraid to ask what he said in response.

I expect Claire to have an answer. She seems like the

kind of girl who could write a guidebook to navigating life at eleven years old. It could be called *Claire's Guide to Cool* or something. She seems confident enough. She tried to get away with not playing tennis at tennis camp. She always says what she thinks.

Though I wish she hadn't said what she thought to Bennett just now.

"I don't know," she says. "I'm sorry. But I think this is for the best."

"Claire." I grab her arm as she's walking away. "I can't go back over there. I'm scared."

"Well, we have dogs to take care of, Remy." She links her arm with mine. "Business is business, babe."

That makes me laugh, and as soon as I'm laughing I can walk back over to them. But when we get to the bench, the giggling stops. Bennett looks at me. And I look at him. We look down at our feet. And no one says anything.

"Do you guys want to take the dogs over to Daisy's for some treats?" Bennett asks after the world's longest pause. "I think they need a change of scenery. We've been here all morning."

"That never bothered them before," I say, more defensively than I'd meant to.

"Well, our boys are bored," Calvin says. He's calling them his boys? He's only been helping out for a few days. "We're gonna take Rascal, Lester, Atticus, and Oscar to Daisy's, and then we'll take them home later."

I look at him, annoyed that he's making this decision.

"That's okay with you, Rem?" Bennett asks. He's smart enough to ask me that. It's my business, not Calvin's.

I nod. "Sure. Fine. Whatever."

They gather the dogs' belongings and head out. I can't help but wonder if Claire's comment made them want to leave. And I can't tell if I'm sad that they're gone or sad that Calvin called those dogs his boys.

I feel cloudy again.

"Well, that wasn't good," Claire says. Tabby, Potato Salad, and Marilyn Monroe are all sunbathing at our feet. It's going to be a very relaxed afternoon.

"What wasn't good?" I ask. I'm only half paying attention.

"The way you acted." She looks at me, and when I don't turn to face her, she puts her hands on the sides of my face and literally turns my head. "If you like him, then just go with it. Don't act all weird and like you don't care. I mean, it's Bennett. You've known him your whole life. Just be who you are."

"I don't know who I am," I say. "It's all so confusing. One of my best friends isn't talking to me. And I think I'm in love with my other one."

"Don't be so dramatic, Remy." She rolls her eyes—something I haven't seen her do in at least a day. "Get out of your head for a few minutes and just be normal."

I know Claire's trying to help, in her way, but this whole debacle has made me exhausted. I just need some quiet time.

The dogs are resting, and I want to rest too. I get up and pull over one of the Dog Beach lounge chairs. Thankfully, there isn't too much fur on it. I decide to lie down for a few minutes.

But I can't really relax. I won't close my eyes, because I need to pay attention to the dogs.

Tabby and Potato Salad get picked up early, and then it's just Claire, Marilyn Monroe, and me.

"Psst," I say to Claire, who's dozing off on the bench.

"What?" she asks.

"I have an idea. Since it's just the three of us, let's do a special trip." She uh-huhs me with her eyes closed. "Let's take her to Mornings."

"What? No! That place is too fancy for dogs." She opens her eyes and raises her eyebrows. "That lady Beverly seriously scares me, and no one scares me. Did you hear she wouldn't even allow her own cousin into the store because he wasn't dressed well enough?"

I glare at her. "She's really mean, but Mornings was Danish's favorite place," I say. "He'd wait outside on their front porch, and I'd bring him a croissant. That's what we'll do. I figured out how to work the system and get around Beverly every time."

"For real?"

"Totally. Just trust me."

"All right, let's do it." Claire smiles.

"You're gonna love this, Mari," I whisper to her as we're

walking over. "It can be our special thing. I wouldn't take just any dog there, but you're different."

She barks softly and wags her tail with her ears perked up. She's excited. She must know something's up.

When we get there, I tell Claire and Marilyn Monroe to wait on the side of the porch so Beverly won't see them. I'll go in and get some croissants and some fresh-squeezed orange juice and be right back.

We have the plan all figured out.

I walk inside and it's crowded, but not as crowded as it is in the morning. The place is called Mornings, so that does make sense.

"Hello, Remy," Beverly says in a not-so-pleased-to-see-me tone. That's kind of how she is with everyone, but especially kids. I think she'd prefer it if Mornings was an adults-only place, but Seagate isn't like that. She's, like, the only mean person on the whole island, but her chocolate croissants are the best in the world. It doesn't make any sense.

"How are you, Beverly?" I ask, all polite, the way my parents taught me.

"Doing well, thanks." She takes my order: I tell her two chocolate croissants and one plain (dogs shouldn't have chocolate), and two fresh-squeezed orange juices and a cup of water. It's all going according to plan, but she does seem to be moving more slowly than usual, and I start to worry. Marilyn Monroe isn't the most patient dog, and I'm pretty sure Claire is even less patient than she is.

Just as I'm digging through my pocket for some money, calculating the total in my head so I can be ready to pay as soon as Beverly comes back to the counter, I hear Claire's raised voice.

Oh no. Hopefully, she tied Marilyn Monroe outside carefully so she can't run away.

And then I hear barking. Marilyn Monroe's unmistakable, high-pitched barking. That bark means that she wants what she wants and she's going to get it and nothing can get in her way. Not even Mornings. Not even mean Beverly. I stand on my tiptoes to look out the window.

Uh-oh.

"Remy! Help!" Claire yells, reaching out for the leash in front of her, but it's too late. Marilyn Monroe is off and running, all around the restaurant, her sea-green hair bow bobbing up and down as she goes. Claire runs into the restaurant and grabs my hand. "She kept looking for you and sniffing around, and maybe she smelled the croissants? Or maybe she missed you. She just took off. Someone opened the door and she took that as her moment and she stormed in, ran through the door, and oh—" She makes a horrified face.

"What?"

"She's sitting on that woman's lap!"

We both look back and see Marilyn Monroe sitting on some fancy lady's lap. The woman doesn't look pleased.

"Remy!" Beverly is yelling now. "Get that dog out of here!"

"Sorry, Beverly. So sorry."

"We do not allow dogs. How many times have I told you that? Think twice before coming back."

I scoop Marilyn Monroe off the woman's lap and apologize a million times. But I don't realize that her right paw is stuck under the tablecloth, so when I lift her up, I get the whole tablecloth at the same time. Iced coffee spills everywhere. Water spreads all over the floor. Eggs end up in laps, pancakes fly in the air, and the beautiful variety croissant basket flops off the table and lands at an angry man's feet.

"Sorry. So sorry."

Claire's just standing there, holding her head with one hand and grabbing my arm with the other. It feels like five hundred years pass before we make it outside. And when we're finally out there, I realize that the croissants we came to get are still on the counter. I guess we'll never get them now.

"Oh my goodness, that was the most horrible few minutes of my whole life," Claire says. "That was so embarrassing."

"We should tell Amber what happened, in case she tries to go there with Marilyn Monroe again."

"Oh my God, Remy, no! It totally wasn't our fault, and it's over now anyway. Let's just take Marilyn Monroe home and forget about it."

I'm speechless.

Claire goes on and on about how the place is dumb, and Beverly is too uptight, and why did we go there? And how it was the stupidest idea ever.

"Claire!" I finally interrupt her. "How could you let her escape?"

"Let her escape? I was using all my power to hold her back." She glares at me and does her signature Claire eye roll, but then I see that she really does feel bad. "I'm sorry, Remy. It was an accident."

I look at Marilyn Monroe. "Any apologies from you, my dear?"

She lets out her little whimper and tries to jump up my leg. I guess she wants me to pick her up. She needs me to comfort her—even though she's the one who acted poorly. Oh well. I can't say no to that face.

On our way back, we see Mason Redmond and Micayla on the bench outside Sundae Best, and Marilyn Monroe tries to break away from us as soon as we see them. She is pretty strong when she sets her mind to something, I'll admit that.

When we get closer, Marilyn Monroe hops up onto Micayla's lap.

Micayla says, "She must've smelled me. I guess she's been missing me as much as I've been missing her." I'm not sure if Micayla is talking to me or to Claire, but I nod anyway.

We tell her and Mason the whole story about the debacle of Marilyn Monroe breaking into Mornings. They don't seem as shocked or amused as they should be.

"You didn't come to Dog Beach today." I look at Mason and notice that he and Micayla are sharing a cherry chip sundae in one cup with two spoons. I wonder if that's his favorite flavor too. If it is, they're meant for each other. I don't know anyone else who likes cherry chip besides Micayla.

"I took the day off," he says. "My boss said it's okay."

"I see." Mason is pretty much his own boss, and he finds this joke very funny.

Claire's just standing next to me, not saying anything—for once.

"Well, I guess we'd better get Marilyn Monroe home," I say. "We're pretty tired from all the stress."

"Okay. Well, bye!" Micayla says, all cheery. I have no idea what she's thinking. All these days have passed, and we haven't talked. I never found out about the tour of Seagate Schoolhouse or the new girl Avery Sanders knew who's also going to school there. I haven't heard how the Mason Sundae Best thing happened. Maybe it was because he took my suggestion. Maybe not. I want to tell Micayla about Bennett and me, and what Claire said, and how I feel about him in general, but clearly now is not the time. We leave Micayla and Mason and take Marilyn Monroe home.

"Well, today has certainly not been boring!" Claire says. She's carrying Marilyn Monroe in her arms. We can't trust her to walk alone anymore today. "Most exciting day on Seagate all summer!"

"Yeah. For you."

"What does that mean?" she asks.

"You're not the one with all these emotional obstacles to

overcome," I say. "And now I'll never be allowed a chocolate croissant from Mornings ever again!"

"First of all, rein it in, Drama Queen Remy. And second of all, I'm sure Beverly will forget by next summer."

"You think?"

"Totally," Claire says.

After we bring Marilyn Monroe back to her house, I walk home quietly, thinking about the day. Tonight's my mom's August book club meeting, and Dad is back from the city, so I'm excited for a quiet night with him.

I realize I was at Sundae Best today but didn't even take the time to get ice cream. I must've been really distracted to forget about ice cream.

I sit down on the rocking chair on our front porch before heading inside for dinner. Maybe Claire's right. I wish we hadn't trashed Mornings, but it was actually kind of funny. It distracted me from the Bennett embarrassment. It was an exciting day, and a little excitement never hurt anyone.

"*Funny seeing you here,*" *Mr. Brookfield says,* zapping me out of my thoughts. I look around and wonder what he means. I'm on my own front porch. Dad and I had a nice dinner together, but all I could think about was getting outside again.

"Huh?"

"I'm kidding, Remy." He winks. "How are things?"

I shrug. "Fine, I guess." I don't feel like getting into any major discussions right now. "Going for an evening stroll?"

He nods. "Of course."

Mr. Brookfield comes to join me on the porch. He starts to tell me all about his Seagate routine—a walk in the morning and a walk at night, with all sorts of things in between— when I start to feel uneasy again.

As exciting as it was, I'm starting to feel guilty about all the trouble Marilyn Monroe caused. I should have stayed back with her, not Claire. And maybe I shouldn't have brought her there in the first place. Marilyn Monroe is awesome, but she's not Danish. She's her own dog, and maybe she's just not Mornings-ready yet.

I don't care what Claire says: I have to tell Amber. I can't keep this huge thing from her and let her find out the hard way, when she's craving a chocolate croissant and a fresh-squeezed OJ and she's turned away without even knowing why. Beverly will probably scream at her and embarrass her, and Amber hates to be embarrassed. She'll be forced to sell her Seagate house and she'll be miserable for the rest of her life.

I guess there I go being Drama Queen Remy again, as Claire would say.

"Doggie Day Camp going well?" Mr. Brookfield asks. He always calls it that, even though I'm not totally sure that's what it is. We should have picked a name right away. If you go too long without naming something, it just goes unnamed. Or people call it what they want to call it.

I nod my head yes. I don't feel like talking. Everything that might come out of my mouth will sound sad or frustrated.

"I heard someone talking about you the other day," Mr. Brookfield says. "I was on my morning walk and two of the ladies from the Seagate Singers were sitting on a bench after practice, gabbing about the group of kids who take care of the Seagate dogs. It was very sweet."

I nod again.

"I'm awfully proud of you, Remy. For all the work with the dogs, and the way you've welcomed my Calvin and my Claire." He looks at me. I try to smile. But then the tears just start pouring out of my eyes.

"Don't be proud of me," I say. "Marilyn Monroe broke into Mornings today and pulled a whole covered tablecloth off. And Micayla's mad at me. And nothing is really as great as it seems."

"What are you talking about?" he asks in his jokey voice, like I'm overreacting.

I tell him the whole story about making Claire and Marilyn Monroe waiting outside Mornings and how Marilyn Monroe just couldn't wait anymore.

"I see" is all he says after that. He's not joking anymore. He's not saying anything at all. Maybe he's waiting for me to continue.

"And I was mean to Micayla. She waited so long to tell me they were becoming year-rounders, and I got so upset that she didn't tell me that I didn't even pay attention to how she was feeling about it. And now things are just strange and angry between us."

Mr. Brookfield sighs and sits back in his chair, like he's about to say something wise. "It happens. My best friend Morris and I once went a whole year without speaking."

"Really? Why?"

"It's hard to remember, Remy. Something about a poker

match and a beef stew and being late for a fortieth birthday party." He smiles. "Eventually we made up. If a friendship is meant to stand the test of time, it will."

"I guess it's like anything else," I start. "An everything-happens-for-a-reason kind of thing."

When I don't say anything else for a few seconds, Mr. Brookfield asks, "And what about Bennett? I haven't seen you two together much lately."

I think hard about how I'm going to answer that, but in the end I just say, "I can't talk about it."

"I understand," he replies. "You don't need to say anything else." I should give him more credit for understanding the way an eleven-year-old thinks. I'm pretty sure he gets it.

I'm glad he doesn't think I need to say anything else, but all of a sudden, I feel so much lighter. I feel relieved. Maybe that's why Claire always says what's on her mind. It's better that way. You don't have to carry these heavy thoughts around with you all the time.

"Things will work out, Remy," Mr. Brookfield says, tying his shoelace. "They always do."

"Thanks. I think I feel a little bit better." I smile.

"Good. I'm glad." He stands up. "Now I must be finishing my evening walk before it's time for my morning one! Good talking to you."

I sit outside for a few more minutes and then realize that I was on cleanup duty for dinner. I only planned to be outside for a minute or two, but then Mr. Brookfield came by, and now those dishes have been sitting in the sink for a little too long.

I go back inside and load the dishwasher, and then I hear a knock on the door. I'm having déjà vu from last month's book club night, when Mom was out and Bennett found Oscar. I put down the stack of dishes and go to the door. And it's not actually déjà vu, but it does seem to be a repeat of last month.

Bennett's at the door.

"Can I talk to you?" he asks.

My heart starts flipping around like a fish desperately trying to get back into the water. I peer back into the kitchen and yell, "Dad, I'll be on the front porch for a minute."

"Again?" he asks from the living room. He gets up and sees Bennett in the doorway. "Oh, um, okay."

"Did you find another lost dog?" I ask Bennett when we're alone on the front porch.

It takes him a second to get what I'm talking about, but then he laughs.

"No. I just feel like we haven't hung out that much since I went on that trip with Calvin. And I'm kind of worried—what's up with you and Micayla?"

I look at him to make sure he's being serious. He usually makes jokes out of "girl fights." But tonight he came over here all on his own. That makes me think that this fight with Micayla is more serious—if even Bennett noticed it, it must be bad.

"I've been hanging out with Claire. And Micayla is hanging out with some year-rounders, I guess. And Mason Redmond." I pause and wonder if I should say what I'm about to say. "You said it yourself that it's okay to have other friends. Didn't you?"

"Remy. Come on."

"What?" I ask, not looking at him.

He sits down on the little bench on the porch. I stay standing, because I don't know if I can handle sitting that close to him right now. I'm too nervous. "Obviously it's okay to have other friends, but you don't just get into fights with your best friends and not make up," he says. "That's really not like you, Remy."

I don't know what to say, so I just keep quiet.

"I told Micayla I was coming here. I told her the same things I told you," he says. "It's freakin' annoying that you two are being babies, so I had to stop it."

"Mediator Bennett!" I say, trying to lighten the tone of this conversation. I finally sit on the edge of the bench with him.

"Well, yeah, and also I have to bail on dog-sitting in two days. Calvin and I signed up for the tennis tournament."

"You finally have a tennis partner," I say. Bennett loves tennis, but Micayla and I never got into it. He's been trying to find a partner for the tournament for years now. I guess I'm happy for him. About that, at least.

"So I need Micayla to get back into the business. We can't both bail on you."

"Well, that's true."

I wonder if I should say anything else, about how he knows that I have all these mixed-up feelings for him. Or maybe he's already forgotten about that, or he doesn't want to talk about it because he doesn't think of me like that.

But I can't bring it up. It doesn't feel like the right time, and I'm way too nervous to talk about that kind of thing. When I can't think of anything else to say, I bring up Mr. Brookfield's scream and how we're still obsessed with it, and also about the other teams participating in the tennis tournament. Just average Seagate stuff. But it feels like there's a cloud hanging in the air between us, not allowing us to have a comfortable conversation. And also, one minute I want to give Bennett a hug, and the next minute I want to push him off the porch.

I'm disappointed about Bennett bailing on dog-sitting, but I'm happy for him about the tournament. And I'm happy that he came over to talk to me.

I decide not to bring up what Claire told him. I think back to what Mr. Brookfield said before about that fight he had with Morris about beef stew and how it lingered on for a whole year. I can't let that happen with Micayla. I have to fix things with her before I tackle anything else.

The next morning, everything seems clearer. I'm not sure why. It's one of those rare mornings when I hop out of bed feeling refreshed and rejuvenated.

I step outside the way I always do first thing in the morning. In the city, you can't just go outside for a second. It's a whole process—going down the hallway, into the elevator, down to the lobby, and outside.

But here I can walk straight out the back door and breathe in the ocean air, still in my pajamas. I never take that for granted. Today, though, the air seems fresher than usual. Maybe it was the talk with Mr. Brookfield, or maybe it was that Bennett stopped by and seemed to actually care about what was happening with Micayla and me. But the combination of everything has given me a whole new outlook.

My mom is in the kitchen making pancakes, and my dad

used our juicer for fresh-squeezed orange juice. I'm not sure what it is, but everything seems delightful.

And as I'm sitting down at the table, eating my mom's famous made-from-scratch pancakes with maple butter on the side, it occurs to me. It's like an epiphany, but an epiphany that's been there the whole time, just waiting for me to realize it.

It's so simple, really. But I know why I've been so mixed up about everything. Because I've been keeping all these confusing feelings to myself. The same way that Mr. Brookfield never really told anyone how much he missed the movies, how he never told anyone that the Scream was a big part of his life.

I need to tell Micayla that the whole year-rounder thing feels like a big change. But the person the change will affect the most is Micayla, not me. And that I'll always be here for her if she wants to talk. And if she doesn't want to talk, that's okay too.

I need to get up the courage and tell Bennett myself how I'm feeling.

And probably the first thing I need to do is be honest with Amber about Marilyn Monroe and Mornings. I'll never feel okay with everything until I fess up about what happened.

After I finish my pancakes, I run upstairs to change into shorts and a T-shirt. But I pack a bathing suit and a towel just in case I find time for a swim later in the day. I really doubt it will happen, since I still have to make up with Micayla, and that could take a while. But on Seagate you should never leave home without a bathing suit. Micayla and I used to swim at least once a day. And then things got busy with the dogs and weird between us. And everything felt different.

Different isn't always bad, though. It's comfortable when things stay the same, but comfortable can also mean boring, and different can also mean exciting. It's all in the way you look at it. Plus, it's not all black and white. Different doesn't have to be totally different; it can be just a little bit different. Like with Calvin and Claire coming this summer. It was still Seagate, just Seagate with a couple additions.

The new days can still be a little bit like the old days, I think, as long as you make room for new traditions too.

I stop at Claire's first to tell her about my plan to talk to Amber. I'm not going to force her to come too, but I want to let her know what I'm doing.

I knock on the door a few times, but no one answers. Finally I decide just to go in. It makes sense that they didn't hear the knocking, because Claire and Mr. Brookfield are sitting on the living room couch listening to the Scream.

"Good morning!" Mr. Brookfield says, all cheerful. "Are you hungry? We have fresh-baked muffins."

"I just had pancakes," I tell them. "But thank you."

Claire pats the couch, so I sit down next to her, and for the next few minutes we just keep listening to the Scream over and over, like we do at our pizza parties. Only this time, there's no talking over it. We're just sitting here quietly.

Mr. Brookfield stops the recording. "Now you're awake, right, Claire?"

She nods. "We started a new morning tradition," she tells me. "We listen to the Scream together. It really wakes us up."

"Yeah. I can imagine."

"It's like a wake-up call to get up from sleeping, and also a wake-up call to start the day and do something extreme," Claire says. "I can't really explain it. So we listen to the Scream, and then we scream!"

"I like it. I think that's really cool."

"Thank you," Mr. Brookfield says. "It's a way to appreciate something old and make it new at the same time." He winks at me.

If I knew how to wink, I would wink back. I hope he knows how much our conversations have changed the way I think about things.

"We have to go tell Amber what happened," I say to Claire. "I can't live with the guilt."

"But MM is fine." Claire widens her eyes at me like I'm a crazy person, and I get the sense that she wants me to keep quiet and not talk about the incident anymore in front of her grandfather. "It wasn't that big of a deal. And Beverly is old; she'll forget about it."

"You know how you just say what's on your mind?" I remind Claire. "Well, I'm trying to be more like that."

There's a moment where we just look at each other. Then Claire nods slowly, all proud of herself. "Well, when you say it like that, I guess I'm in. I'll be down in a minute."

She runs up the stairs, and I sit on Mr. Brookfield's couch and look at his collection of tiny director's chairs.

"Feeling any better about things?" he asks me, picking up his mug of steaming coffee.

I shrug. "Maybe a little bit. I'm going to think about the Scream wake-up call. Maybe I need something like that in my life too."

"You can join us anytime," he says. "It's done wonders for my little Claire."

He's right about that. When I think about Claire at the beginning of the summer and of her now, she seems like a completely different person. Her surly, angry personality has been washed away.

She's still honest—she says whatever's on her mind, even if it's rude or embarrassing. But her attitude has changed.

Maybe the Seagate air was a remedy for her grumpiness, or maybe it was quality time with her grandfather. I'm not sure. But the new Claire is way better than the old Claire. I guess that's an example of change being a really good thing.

Claire and I walk over to Marilyn Monroe's house totally silently. I wonder if she's as nervous as I am.

"Hi, girls, you here to get Mari?" Amber asks, greeting us at the door. She's in yoga pants, with some kind of workout video on the TV behind her. "You're early. Didn't we say noon?"

"Yeah. We, um, I mean, I wanted to talk to you for a second," I tell her.

"Sure. Come in."

Amber turns off the workout DVD and sits with us on the couch. Hudson's toys are thrown all around the room. Marilyn Monroe is sleeping under the kitchen table, and I know how much she values her naps. It would be nice to pet her right now, but I don't want to wake her up.

"I'm sorry I didn't tell you this last night," I start. "But Marilyn Monroe sort of broke into Mornings yesterday, and Beverly's really mad about it, and you probably can't ever go back there with Marilyn Monroe again. We probably shouldn't have taken her there, but we thought it would be a special treat. I used to do it all the time with my dog, Danish. Anyway, I guess she was so excited, she just stormed in and hopped up onto an old lady's lap and then ripped the tablecloth off. Well, maybe that was my fault, because it happened when I tried to take her off the lady's lap. Actually, maybe it's all my fault, because I shouldn't have taken her there in the first place."

"I see." Amber pauses to think for a minute, looking a little bit confused. But then after a long moment she starts laughing. Really laughing. Claire cracks up next. And then I start laughing too. When one of us laughs, we both laugh. Usually uncontrollably.

"My Mari wants what she wants. She's an independent woman," Amber says. "I'm disappointed she stormed in, but I'm glad you told me."

"I'm really sorry," I say again.

"Me too," Claire adds.

"I know, and I appreciate that." Amber smiles. "We all make mistakes. Once, I left my son behind at the yoga studio. He was napping in the back room, and I just left without him." She shakes her head like she can't believe how dumb she was. "I never told my husband," she whispers.

"I'm trying to be more honest," I tell her. "And not hide my feelings so much."

Claire nudges me with her arm and gives me a look that says I'm talking too much and Amber doesn't want to hear this.

I guess there's a balance, and I haven't found it yet.

But we sit and talk with Amber for a little while longer, and she tells us that she still gets in fights with her friends. I'm not sure if that's supposed to make us feel better or worse, but it's interesting to hear about.

We end up taking Marilyn Monroe a little early and then going to pick up Oscar and Atticus. Bennett and Calvin are picking up the others today.

"That was easier than I thought," Claire says.

"You didn't say anything!"

"Yeah, I mean, easier for you." She grins. "So your next project is . . . ?"

"Micayla. I have to fix things with Micayla," I say. "Let's take the dogs and stop at her house. You can wait outside. I can't have you laughing and distracting me."

"Fair enough," Claire says. "My laugh is pretty powerful."

She bursts into some weird Wicked Witch of the West laugh, and we both crack up again.

Maybe Claire changed. Or maybe I changed. Or maybe we both did. Regardless, I don't know how it's possible that I ever hated her.

On the walk to Micayla's, my head is full of ideas.
Ideas about what I'm going to say to her to make things right,
ideas about how I'll eventually talk to Bennett. And an idea
for Mr. Brookfield too. Claire and Mr. Brookfield's new morning Scream tradition made me think of it, and I want to tell
Claire, but I'm worried she'll think it's dumb. And she's not
afraid to tell me when she thinks something's dumb.

We're friends now, but I'm still a little scared of her. That
makes sense, though. I don't think people could ever change
completely, if we'd even want them to.

"I just timed it," she says, breaking me out of my thoughts.

"Timed what?"

Claire looks at me, but I don't meet her gaze. "The amount
of time you've been silent. One minute, eight seconds. Something must be on your mind. So spill."

I don't say anything right away.

"Oh Lordy," she groans. "Not again. I thought you were done with being keep-things-to-yourself Remy. I thought you were going to speak your mind now!"

I laugh. "Okay. Promise you'll have an open mind?"

"Suuuuure," she says, sounding reluctant.

"Well, do you know about Seagate Halloween?" I ask.

"Remy, it's only August."

I nod. "Yeah, I know. But Seagate Halloween is Labor Day weekend. It's a huge tradition. There's a big parade and people dress up and then we eat all the candy we can. That's it. No trick-or-treating or anything."

"So it's basically a big costume party?" Claire asks.

"Yeah. But the best costume party you've ever been to."

Claire bends down to clean up after Oscar. "So what's your idea?"

"Well, here's the thing. For all the past years, we did Seagate Halloween exactly the same. Same costumes, same traditions, everything the same. And that was kind of what made it so awesome."

"Uh-huh."

"Well, I've realized that things can't always stay the same. We're forced to change. And I think we can make a new addition to Seagate Halloween!"

"Oh-kay." Claire looks nearly ready to roll her eyes. I need to get to the point.

"Here's the idea: Your grandpa starts the parade with

his scream. We make a little introduction and tell everyone who he is, and then he screams! I thought about adding the Scream to the Sandcastle Contest, but this makes way more sense."

"Go on."

"He and I had this whole talk about bringing your past into your present but not too much and not dwelling on it and all that." I start speed-talking, a little afraid Claire will shoot down my idea before I say it all. "And I think this is exactly in that spirit! Old things and new traditions! And it's Halloween, so a scream fits!"

I hold my breath and wait to hear what she'll say.

"I like it," Claire says. "It'll be like he's a celebrity finally."

"Good. As long as you're on board, we can make it happen!"

"Well, I don't know about that. But okay." She pauses for a second. "I have an idea to add to your idea. Ready?"

I nod.

"Y'know how every Sunday on Seagate they show movies on the lawn behind the stadium?"

"Uh-huh."

"So maybe in the weeks leading up to Seagate Halloween, they can show scary movies, the ones with my grandpa's scream." She looks at me, and I swear this must be the most excited I've seen her since the day she showed me her new jeans. "And then people can hear it, and they'll recognize it at the parade. And then they'll realize that he really is famous!"

"I love it. I love it. I love it!" I jump up and down and grab Claire's hands, and soon we're jumping up and down together like people who have just won the lottery.

We get to Micayla's house, and I feel like I'm bursting apart with excitement. I'm going to make things right with Micayla and Bennett. And then Claire and I are going to make Mr. Brookfield the star of Seagate, which he is already, even though nobody knows. Everyone's going to hear his scream in those movies, and everyone is going to know how amazing he is.

Claire tells me she's going to take the dogs and meet Bennett and Calvin at Dog Beach, and that Micayla and I should come when we're done.

"Hi, Rem," Micayla's mom says when she opens the door. "I've missed you."

"Same," I say. "I have to talk to Micayla. Is she here?"

"Yup. Go on up."

Micayla's sister, Ivy, is sitting on their living room couch looking at the computer. She does one of those backward waves, not turning around. I wave back, even though she can't see me.

Micayla has her door open, and before she even sees me, I peer in and notice that her room looks completely different. For one thing, she has a desk in it now. She never needed a desk before, but I guess some of the furniture from their house was moved here already.

She's sitting on her bed looking at magazines. I don't want to startle her, so I knock gently.

"Remy!" she yelps. I guess I startled her anyway. Maybe there was no way of avoiding it.

"Micayla, I'm so sorry." I say it right away. I need her to know that's why I'm here. "I should have been more supportive and understanding of this whole big change in your life. I should have been a better friend."

"Well, thanks. But you're not good with change." She smiles her soft Micayla smile. "You're always talking about tradition and wanting everything to be the same, year after year. I guess maybe that's why I didn't want to tell you. I felt like if my life changed, it would let you down."

"But it's your life, not mine." I sit down on the edge of her bed. I realize we haven't had a sleepover all summer. Are we too old for sleepovers? I hope not. I don't think that you can ever really get too old for sleepovers. I mean, even when you're married, it's pretty much like a sleepover every night.

"That's true," Micayla says.

"It hurt my feelings that you'd keep a big secret from me. And then I guess I just got worried that I was being replaced by Avery Sanders. She's nice and everything, but . . . you know."

Micayla shakes her head. "You're not being replaced. I promise."

"Good." I smile.

"Anyway, I forgive you. I miss you too much to not forgive you."

"I missed you so much too." I reach across and give her a

hug. "Why did your parents decide to become year-rounders? I never even asked you that."

She sighs. "You mean aside from the fact that Seagate Island is the best place on earth?"

I laugh. "Yeah. Aside from that."

"Well, we just don't need the big house in New Jersey anymore, since Zane and Ivy are away at college. It feels really empty when they're away. And my parents started wondering why they were paying for two places when they'd rather just be here." She shrugs. "I don't know. That's what they said. And we're all so happy on Seagate, it just made sense."

"I bet it's going to be great," I tell her, because it seems like the right thing to say. And then I feel even guiltier for not being more supportive before. This was likely a big decision for them, not something they just decided in a few minutes. And it probably will be great—just because it's not the Seagate I know doesn't mean it's not still Seagate.

"Oh! I still have to tell you about Mason Redmond," Micayla says.

"Oh yeah!"

"I think we, like, *like* each other," she says.

"*Like* like?" I giggle. "Really? How do you know?"

She twists a few braids around her finger. "We had fun at Sundae Best. And his favorite flavor is also cherry chip. And we had a lot to talk about." She pauses. "He's not always thinking about his future, you know. I mean, he is, in that he signed up to play lacrosse this year, but that's it."

"That's good. So what happens now?"

"No clue." She gets up and grabs the hoodie off her desk chair. "But it's fun. Do I look okay?" She turns around and poses. "We're going to Dog Beach now, right?"

"Yeah." I smile. "You look beautiful."

On our walk over to Dog Beach, I tell Micayla about my idea for Mr. Brookfield's scream and Seagate Halloween.

"I love it!" She high-fives me. "So smart. Halloween is all about screaming!"

"I know, right?" I throw up my hands. "It just came to me. And hey, there's something else we need to talk about."

Micayla looks at me sideways. "Bennett, right?"

"How did you know?"

"Come on, Rem. You totally like him. It's, like, the oldest story in the world—girls fall in love with their best friends all the time."

"They do?" I ask. "How do you know?"

She gives me an are-you-serious look. "I just know. And also, Ivy told me she was in love with her best friend from home for three years."

"I don't know what to say," I admit. "I don't know exactly what happened. I just know that things changed. He's not just plain old Bennett anymore with the ratty T-shirts and the untied shoelaces who always burns the top of his mouth when eating pizza."

"Well, he still is that Bennett, but maybe you just see something else too?" Micayla asks.

"Yeah. I guess that's it. He's still the same, but there's kind of more to him, or more underneath that only I can see. I can't explain it."

Micayla nods. "I get what you're saying."

"So what do I do?"

"*That* I don't know."

"That's exactly what Claire said," I tell her.

"Claire gives you advice now?" she asks, raising an eyebrow.

"Sometimes. But don't worry, you haven't been replaced or anything."

"I know I can't be replaced. I'm not worried."

"We didn't even talk about Seagate Schoolhouse and Avery Sanders and all that," I say. "We got off track. Tonight: you and me, sleepover and s'mores. Sound good?"

"Sounds perfect."

The rest of the day at Dog Beach goes well. Everyone's happy to be there. Calvin and Bennett keep a game of Frisbee going for more than an hour. Marilyn Monroe is happy traipsing around from Micayla to Claire to me to all the other dogs.

Tabby and Potato Salad are lazy as usual, but they push a ball back and forth with their noses, and it's so cute that I take a video of it with my phone. I'm convinced it's going to be the next YouTube sensation.

It feels weird without Lester here, but they were only doing a short-term rental. Maybe he'll be back next summer.

If I were to give out awards, I think I'd give him "most social dog."

I keep watching Mason and Micayla to see what it's like when two people like each other. I don't really notice anything that crazy. They laugh often and smile all the time and have tons to say to each other, but that's it as far as I can tell.

"Things are okay with you guys?" Claire asks me when Micayla's at the lifeguard's chair.

"Really okay," I say. I almost tell her about the sleepover, but I don't want to make her feel left out, and I also don't know if I should include her. Perhaps Micayla and I need some one-on-one time. "Now I just have one more big idea. We need to finish our day here so I can talk to your grandpa and then I can talk to Mrs. Paisley tomorrow, the one who handles all the planning for Seagate Halloween."

"So come over after we drop the dogs off," Claire says. "I think your boyfriend and my brother are going out for burgers with my dad."

"Oh, your dad's back?" I ask.

"Yeah, my mom leaves and he comes back. I don't know what that's all about."

Suddenly the tone of the conversation goes cloudy, and I don't know if I should ask any more questions.

"Probably just schedules," Claire says. "They're confusing. I try not to think about it too much."

"Aren't grown-ups mysterious?" I ask, trying to make a joke. "They can drive and they have jobs and bank accounts and stuff. But then sometimes you'll ask them the reason for something and they'll just say because they said so. And then you realize they don't have anything figured out at all."

"Exactly." Claire shakes her head. "They're all cuckoo."

"Mr. Brookfield, I have the best idea!" I yell, running into the house. Claire and I find him sitting in his armchair reading a thick book with a dark, spooky cover.

"Yes, Remy?"

"You will be the voice of Seagate Halloween! You know how everyone dresses up and we have the parade and everything?"

"Of course!"

"Well, your scream will start the whole thing. Kind of like a fanfare on a trumpet or a whistle." I put my hands on my hips. "What do you think?"

"I'm in!" He winks. "Isn't that what all the young people say these days?"

Claire and I crack up, and Bennett and Calvin do too. They're hanging over the railing listening to our whole conversation. It's surprising that Mr. Brookfield didn't need much convincing, but maybe he's been waiting for this all along.

Claire tells him all about her idea to show scary movies during the Seagate Sunday night movies.

"I'll talk to Mrs. Paisley," I tell him.

"We'll go together," Mr. Brookfield says. "I've known her for years."

"She's always at Breakfast by the Boardwalk in the morning," I say, even though he probably already knows that. "Let's meet her there tomorrow. Claire, you come too."

"I'm in," she says, laughing.

In the end, I don't invite Claire to the sleepover, but I think it's okay, because she said she was excited for a Claire-Grandpa date. They were going to Frederick's Fish and then seeing a movie at Seagate Cinema after. I think Claire likes time alone with her grandfather. She hasn't really said it out loud, but I can tell.

I walk home more quickly than I think I've ever walked on Seagate. It's as if my excitement is carrying me and making me walk faster. I can't wait for Seagate Halloween. I can't wait for Mr. Brookfield to scream and for all of Seagate to hear it. Everyone will want to know his story. And he'll be so happy to tell it. His past will become a part of his present and his future, and he'll finally be the celebrity he was meant to be.

The only thing I am still trying to figure out is Bennett.

What should I say to him? On the one hand, I think he already knows. I mean, I know he knows, because Claire told him, but I don't know what he thinks about it. And things are still okay with us. And maybe I shouldn't make anything muddy, since I don't even know what my feelings really mean. But on the other hand, I feel like I'm bursting with feelings, like I'm carrying balloons under my shirt and I have to let them out.

I run through the door and say, "Mom, Micayla's sleeping over!"

My mom comes out from the kitchen and smiles, unsurprised, and I realize she already knows. I guess Micayla's mom told her. And my mom seems so happy, and I'm relieved that this fight—the longest one of our friendship—is over.

"Do you think you're going to want pizza? Or should I make baked ziti? Or what?" my mom asks. She has her painting apron on, and there's a speck of purple paint on her cheek.

"Let's see when Micayla gets here. She just went home to grab her stuff."

I run up to my room and straighten up. Even though Micayla has been here a million times, I feel like tonight is different. It's the beginning of our friendship after the Fight. We have so much to talk about—Seagate Schoolhouse and Mason and Bennett and the dogs.

I look around my room, and for the first time in my whole life, I want to change the decor. I want to take down my old posters, the ones of sunsets and puppies and old-fashioned ice cream parlors. I want to spruce things up. Maybe Mom and I can redecorate—paint over this lavender and make the room a cool sea green or something. Or maybe Mom and I can paint a mural. Mom will have to do all the hard painting, but I can help a little bit.

I want to take out my old gingham beanbag chairs and put in something cool—a director's chair like Mr. Brookfield has, or maybe even some kind of indoor chaise longue.

I don't know what's come over me. Maybe it's that I'm so excited for the future that I want to get it started right away. I'm looking forward to all the possibilities, and I want to be ready for them. I don't want to hang on to old pieces of the past just because they're comfortable and they've always been there.

I want to start fresh and embrace what's coming.

"Remy!" I hear someone yelling from downstairs, so I throw the last of my dirty laundry into the hamper and run down. Micayla's on the porch, grinning.

"Let's get sandwiches at Pastrami on Rye and then have a picnic on the beach behind your house," Micayla says. "We haven't been to the deli since June!"

"I can't believe it," I say, grabbing my bag from the foyer table. "Mom, do you want anything from the deli?"

"Ooh," Mom says, walking in, this time with some yellow paint above her eyebrow. When I say she gets into a painting, I really mean it. "I'd love turkey with coleslaw and Russian dressing."

"You got it." She hands me money and I give her a hug, and soon Micayla and I are off on our walk—like the old days, but even better.

"You're never going to believe who my teacher is," Micayla says.

"Who?"

"Paul. Atticus's owner."

"I thought he was a college professor?" I ask. "And that he's working on his dissertation, or whatever it's called."

"He was. He is. But he's taking a year off and staying on Seagate, and he got a job teaching sixth-grade English." She shakes her head. "But guess why he's staying."

"Um?" I look at her and try to think of the craziest reason ever. "He needs Sundae Best all year long?"

"He's dating Andi! Rascal's owner's daughter. Remember?"

I think back to earlier in the summer. We don't see the owners as much anymore, since one of us just runs into each house to pick up the dog. We never really stay to chat.

"Oh yeah, the yoga one? And her mom had hip surgery?" It's all coming back to me now.

"Yeah, they started talking when they picked up their dogs from us on Dog Beach. The dogs brought them together!" Micayla says, all excited. "Or I guess *we* brought them together!"

"Andi's staying all year too? To teach yoga?" I ask.

"And to help her mom," Micayla reminds me. "And because she's in loooove."

We both start laughing and decide that we're starving and we need to race to Pastrami on Rye.

This is going to be the best sleepover ever.

It's amazing what a sleepover with Micayla Wal-
cott can do. It's basically a miracle panacea—it can cure
anything. That's what Micayla is for me. We stayed up until
two in the morning, had a beach bonfire, played truth or
dare (mostly just truth, actually), and talked and talked and
talked.

So what if she's a year-rounder now? So she'll be on Seagate when I'm not. She's still Micayla and I'm still Remy. And
yeah, things change, but deeper things stay the same. That's
a relief.

We're on our way to Breakfast by the Boardwalk to meet
with Mrs. Paisley and Mr. Brookfield, and then we're going
to pick up the dogs. I can't wait to observe Paul and Andi in
action. Lovebirds in love because of their dogs. Can you get
a better story than that? I don't think so.

When Micayla and I get there, Claire, Mr. Brookfield, and Mrs. Paisley are already there.

"Don't worry, Bennett and Calvin are with the dogs," Claire says, running up to us. "Oscar's mom had to take the triplets for an early pediatrician appointment, so Bennett went to get him, and Calvin decided to pick up Marilyn Monroe on the way."

"Awesome." I smile. "Thanks, Claire."

"Just didn't want you to panic." She looks at Micayla and then back at me. "You two are okay again? Back to being BFFs?"

We nod.

"Thank goodness. That was getting so annoying," Claire adds, rolling her eyes.

We all join Mr. Brookfield and Mrs. Paisley at the table, and Callie, one of the waitresses, brings over hot chocolates and the bakery basket.

"So tell me about this mysterious scream," Mrs. Paisley says, leaning over, her hands folded on the table. "And how come I've never heard about it? Don, I've known you for thirty years."

"I know." Mr. Brookfield laughs, picking a croissant out of the basket. "I guess I always figured no one would care."

"I care, Don." Mrs. Paisley smiles, and it's funny that she keeps calling him Don. I never even knew his first name.

So Mr. Brookfield tells her the story, and she keeps saying "Wow" and "Incredible" and "You're famous."

As he's telling the story, I get a new idea, and it's genius.

I wanted Mr. Brookfield to be the voice and mascot and announcer of Seagate Halloween, but I don't think that's enough. I think everyone needs to scream!

"So what's your idea, Remy?" Mrs. Paisley asks. I quickly whisper to Claire that I just had a major epiphany and am making a slight change to the original idea. I want her to be prepared, because she's a major inspiration for my idea.

I tell them my old idea and they seem intrigued, so I know they'll love my new idea. "And the best part will be a Seagate Scream Contest!"

Claire looks at me and smiles, but it's actually more than a smile. It's more like she's beaming in this super proud way. Her face looks different from how I've ever seen it before, and I almost want to take a picture so that I can show her how happy she looks.

You don't really know what pride looks like until you see it on someone else.

She tells them her idea about the Sunday night scary movies, and Mr. Brookfield's eyes light up. I bet he'll just sit quietly in the back while people watch, not making a big deal out of it at all.

"Well, I love all of this. We'll start showing the Sunday night movies next week," Mrs. Paisley suggests.

"Great!" Micayla says. "We can make posters telling people about the Scream. And everyone will want to know more about it and get even more excited."

We spend the rest of breakfast going over how Mr. Brookfield should dress and where he should sit and who should introduce him and all these other exciting logistics.

To be honest, even though I love Seagate Halloween so much, it always made me a little bit sad because it's over Labor Day weekend, the last weekend of the summer, and that means the end of Seagate for me until next summer.

But this summer, it feels different. I'm excited about it. It almost makes the end of summer tolerable.

It's funny how you can want something to stay the same so, so badly, but then little changes happen, and you realize how great the new thing can be.

When we walk up to Rascal's house later that morning, we notice that Atticus is on the front lawn. Paul and Andi are sitting on the front porch, next to each other on a wicker love seat, while the dogs chase each other.

"Look at them," I say softly to Claire and Micayla.

"Totally in love," Claire says.

"Rascal and Atticus could be stepbrothers very soon!" Micayla laughs. "Stepdogs!"

We all start laughing, and that's when Andi and Paul notice us.

"They're ready for you," Paul says. "Can you watch them until about five today?"

"Sure," I say, putting their leashes on and making a note of the time change.

"Great." Andi smiles. "We're going on a day trip to the wineries in Ocean Edge."

"Sounds fun," Claire says, and when I look up, I notice that Andi and Paul are holding hands. Our little doggie day care is a matchmaker!

We spend the rest of the day with all our dogs—Marilyn Monroe, Oscar, Rascal, Atticus, Tabby, Potato Salad, and Palm.

Everyone's happy. Claire, Micayla, and I sit on the side and people-watch and dog-watch and take everything in. Bennett and Calvin engage in the longest game of Frisbee in Dog Beach history. Then we all go to Ping-Pong and watch a few games, the dogs happily sitting on the side and watching too. And then we get the biggest table at Daisy's and enjoy breakfast for dinner.

All of us together. It's hard to imagine things getting any better than this.

But every time I look at Bennett, I get a flickery feeling— like someone turning a light switch on and off really fast.

It's not exactly a bad feeling, just a new and strange one. But I've realized that sometimes great things come from new and different. Just look at Claire—she didn't want to be here, and I didn't want her here, and now we're friends. I never expected it, and I pretty much resisted it, but it happened, and now I can't imagine Seagate without her.

The next two weeks fly by. Either we're busy with the dogs or we're busy getting ready for Seagate Halloween. Micayla and I have sleepovers pretty much every other night, to make up for all the nights we missed this summer. Claire sometimes comes too.

In addition to getting Mr. Brookfield ready for his new role, we're in charge of getting costumes for all the dogs, and we'll be the ones walking them in the doggie part of the parade.

Rascal and Atticus are going as Ping-Pong players—we're strapping Ping-Pong paddles to their backs. Marilyn Monroe and Tabby are going as Superwoman and Princess Leia. Oscar and Potato Salad are wearing matching doggie tuxedos. Palm is going as a Frisbee, since he's so little. We're basically strapping a Frisbee to him and hoping people get it.

We're trying to get them all into their costumes now so

that we can do a run-through before the parade tomorrow. It's a tough job, but someone's gotta do it. We don't want them to be totally caught off guard tomorrow.

The tuxedos are my favorite of all the costumes, and I kind of wanted Rascal and Atticus to wear them too. But Calvin and Bennett were set on some of the dogs being Ping-Pong players.

"Come on, Rem," Bennett said. "They love to watch the games, and Ping-Pong is a Seagate tradition. It would be weird to leave it out."

I agreed but am kind of regretting it. The tuxedos are just so cute.

Finally, after wrangling and twisting and bribing the dogs with treats, we have them all in their costumes. They're running around Dog Beach that way, and it's pretty much the most adorable thing I've ever seen.

We return the dogs home later with their costumes and tell their owners to make sure they're ready to go at eleven tomorrow. We want to get them prepared for the parade before everyone else gets there at noon.

That night, Micayla, Claire, and I have a sleepover at Micayla's house. Her mom makes us bouyon, an amazing St. Lucian dish that's a sort of stew, and homemade peanut butter cookies. We all sleep in sleeping bags on Micayla's screened-in back porch, even though her room is cozy and nice.

We want to make the most of one of our last nights here and sleep by the sea.

"So what's going on with you and Mason?" Claire asks Micayla.

"I dunno." She laughs nervously. "He's leaving tonight."

"What?"

"Yeah. His sister is starting college. So they had to go back to Philadelphia to get her all settled," Micayla says. "I said good-bye. He said to say good-bye to you guys too."

"He's missing Seagate Halloween!" I yell. "And all the dogs."

"I know." Micayla sighs. "But it's okay. There's always next summer."

I look at Micayla and am amazed by her attitude. But she's right. One of the best things about summer on Seagate is that there's always a next summer to look forward to.

"And what about you?" Claire asks me. "Are you ever going to say anything to Bennett? Or no? And do you guys feel replaced by my brother?"

"A little," I say. "But it's okay. Bennett needed a guy friend."

"You're just going to let the summer end and not say anything?" Claire asks. She seems so serious and concerned, it's making me feel uneasy. I kind of like my friendship with Bennett the way it is. We're friends. And I have a little-more-than-friends feeling about him. But that's okay.

It makes me wonder about Claire, though. Maybe she has a secret, and she's worried about keeping it inside until next summer.

"I'm okay with waiting until next summer," I admit. "I don't want to mess anything up."

"You won't, Rem," Micayla says and puts her arm around me. "Honestly. It's Bennett. He'll love you forever, no matter what."

"Yeah." I go over to the table and take another cookie. "Love me like a friend, like his sister."

"Well, I'm not so sure about that," Claire says. Her eyes have this strange twinkle, and I get the feeling that she wants to tell me something but she's not totally sure that she should.

Micayla and Claire move closer together on the couch. It's getting chilly out here, the way it always does at the end of August. It feels like summer is tired and needs a rest and can't handle being so hot anymore. It's breezier and colder, and we spend most of our afternoons in sweatshirts.

"We need hot chocolate," Micayla tells us, and she hops up from the couch to go and get it. I sit on the back porch with Claire, who now has her sweatshirt hood covering her head and most of her face.

I want to ask her what she's hiding, but I'm also kind of happy to have stopped the Bennett discussion. I don't know how I feel, and sometimes it's okay to admit that you don't know. It feels better that way. It feels like it's protecting me from doing the wrong thing.

"Remy, we have to tell you something," Micayla says when she comes back from the kitchen with a tray of steamy mugs of hot chocolate. I guess Claire and Micayla had a secret conversation at some point and I didn't realize it.

My heart starts pounding. It's happening, and I can't believe I haven't realized it until now. What if Claire loves Bennett and Bennett loves Claire and this has been going on all summer and I didn't even notice? What if that's why Claire told Bennett, so she could figure out if he liked her?

I don't want to know. I don't want to know.

"Bennett likes you," Claire says. "Really, really likes you."

"What?" I ask.

"I mean, okay, he doesn't love you like he's going to propose or anything. I mean, you're eleven," Claire continues. "But he likes you in a different way than he likes us. He slept over the other night. And I was in the bathroom brushing my teeth. My loser brother and Bennett were in my grandpa's upstairs den, and they were playing some dumb video game where they have to get robots into hot-air balloons. My brother might need an intervention, given how obsessed he is with computers and video games. But anyway—"

"Yeah?" I ask. My heart is racing. I can't look at Claire and I can't look at Micayla. I stare at the fraying cushion on Micayla's outdoor chair. I pick at the threads.

"And Bennett goes, 'Remy loves hot-air balloons.' And then my dumb brother goes, 'You've mentioned Remy, like, a million times tonight, dude.'"

Micayla starts laughing. "Your brother has a way of saying things. Have you noticed that?"

"Yeah. Always." Claire rolls her eyes. "And then Bennett basically said that he hadn't mentioned you that much, but then Calvin said he had, and then Bennett said, 'I guess I did. I dunno. She's pretty awesome.'"

Claire sips her mug of hot chocolate. "And then they went back to playing their game."

I don't want to feel or act too excited, because all that means is that he thinks I'm awesome, but I have to admit that it makes me happy. My heart finally calms down, and I smile and sit back on the frayed outdoor chair.

"Thanks for telling me that, Claire," I say. "You didn't have to."

"Of course I didn't have to. Duh." Claire eats another cookie. "But I wanted to. I thought you should know. Because even if you don't say anything, you can go home and spend the year knowing that Bennett thinks you're awesome. And yeah, that's a nice thing to know."

We spend the rest of the night chatting and thinking about the parade tomorrow.

Instead of sleeping on the back porch like we'd planned, we bring our sleeping bags down to the beach and sleep on the sand.

"It's good to have the ocean at our sleepover," Claire tells us. "That's something I never thought I'd say. But it's really true."

Micayla's mom makes us waffles for breakfast, and then we all head home to shower and get ready for Seagate Halloween. Micayla and Bennett came up with this awesome idea that all of us—Micayla, Claire, Calvin, Bennett, and I—should dress up as what Danish and I used to be for Seagate Halloween. So a few of us are beach pails and a few of us are shovels. Micayla's mom and my mom are both super crafty, so they were able to make the costumes for us out of cardboard boxes, papier-mâché, and paint.

I couldn't believe they thought of it, and that Claire and Calvin were excited about it too. Sometimes people will surprise you and do something so nice that it almost seems magical. Sometimes you don't even realize that people care that much about you, even though they've been caring all along.

"Is your grandpa nervous?" I ask Claire when Micayla and I get to her house. We walked over to pick up Claire and Calvin and then we'll all get Bennett together. "I mean, it's pretty much his first performance in—what? Fifty years?"

"I think so," Claire says. "He doesn't seem nervous. More like excited."

"What's his costume?"

"He dressed as Calvin!" She laughs. "I helped him order a pair of trendy jeans online, and he popped the collar of his polo shirt. He's even trying to spike his hair! And he's going to carry an iPad Mini! It's so funny."

Micayla and I crack up. "Calvin hasn't seen him getting ready?" I ask.

"No. He's totally oblivious."

Calvin comes out, barely able to walk in his red beach pail costume, and he high-fives us. "We look awesome," he says.

I look at Claire and Calvin, and I truly can't believe how different they are from how they were at the beginning of the summer. I wonder if they realize how different they are, and if they will always stay this way.

Are they going to be Seagate summer folk forever now? Or will they go home and forget about this summer and how amazing it was? I hope they always remember, and I really think they will. I know I will.

I'm pretty sure that once you're a Seagater, you stay that way for life. And all my life, I was convinced that every Seagate summer had to be exactly like the one before it—with all the same traditions and foods and routines. Now I know that's not true. Businesses can be formed, new people can join the group, anything can happen. Who knows—maybe I'll even pick a new favorite Sundae Best flavor next summer. Crazier things have happened.

Bennett is already waiting for us outside his house. He's playing catch with Asher, who is dressed as a baseball player.

"We're all going as baseball players," Asher tells us. "My whole bunk from camp. Even the girls!"

"Wow," I say. I've barely seen Asher all summer, and he suddenly seems taller and chattier and more mature. He's going over to the parade with the rest of his bunk from camp, so we say good-bye and our group of shovels and pails walks (or hobbles) down there together.

We must look so silly, but it doesn't even bother me. People say that cliques are bad, and they are in many ways, but sometimes it just feels so good to be part of a group. Earlier in the summer, I had no interest in Calvin and Claire joining our trio, but now it feels like they really belong, like they've been here since the beginning.

Bennett taps me on the shoulder. He and Calvin were walking a few feet behind us. "Are you sad about Danish today?"

"Not really. I'm excited to see all our dogs in the parade. And the fact that we're all wearing his costume kind of makes it feel like he's here with us." I adjust the cardboard on my back. "Thanks for asking, though," I say, because it really was sweet that Bennett was concerned about me missing Danish.

I know people say that no one is perfect, but maybe Bennett is. I mean, sure, he said that thing about needing to have more than two friends, and some space from us, and stuff. But most of the time, he's so nice and caring. He notices things about me and remembers them later. That's pretty amazing.

We get to the boardwalk right in front of Dog Beach, and all the dogs are waiting for us. They look great in their costumes.

"I am so excited for this," Dawn, Oscar's mom, says, pushing her superpowered triplet stroller back and forth. "You guys are seriously the best."

"They're superstars," Amber, Marilyn Monroe's mom, says. "Remy, may I please speak with you for a moment?"

"Um, sure," I reply.

We walk over to one of the benches and Amber says, "Listen, Remy, you and Mari developed quite a bond this summer. We're moving to a new apartment this year, and it was a huge decision that I really struggled with, but the building doesn't allow dogs. It's getting harder and harder for me to watch both Hudson and Mari, and we were going to give her to my mom, but now that I'm thinking about it . . ."

Her voice trails off, and I wonder what's going to come next.

"Would you consider adopting her? I mean, if your parents say it's okay? We could still visit. We both live in Manhattan and we're both on Seagate every summer. I just figured, y'know, because she really loves you, and you're dogless now, and . . . you know."

It seems like it's hard for her to say this, so I just keep nodding and saying, "Yeah," and nodding again. I need to ask my parents, but of course! It's Marilyn Monroe! "Of course, I'd love to. More than anything!"

We walk together for a few minutes, talking it over. I'll ask my parents as soon as the parade is over. I hope they say yes!

Andi and Paul are sitting next to each other on the bench that Mr. Brookfield usually sits on. They're sipping coffees and holding hands, and the dogs are at their feet. It's almost too cute to handle.

We round up all the dogs and head over to the stage, where the parade will be starting. Mr. Brookfield is hiding backstage until two minutes before, because he doesn't want anyone to see him. He may also be doing this because he's nervous, but I'm not really sure.

I run over to him and whisper, "You're going to be great, Mr. Brookfield. I mean, you're already great!"

"Thanks, Remy." He pats me on the shoulder. "You're not so bad yourself."

We quickly high-five, and I rejoin the group.

The Pooch Parade is always the first part of Seagate Halloween. I think it's because dogs are such an important part of life here. And they're treated like real Seagate citizens too.

From a dog-friendly restaurant like Daisy's to their own beach, it's clear that they're valued here. Seagate life wouldn't be the same without dogs. Everyone knows it.

And that's what makes it even crazier that there was never a doggie day camp before this summer. It's like it's been on the tip of everyone's tongue for years. I guess I'm just so grateful that it happened. And that we were the ones to make it happen.

"You guys ready?" Mrs. Paisley asks us. We're all lined up with the dogs, and the parade is set to start in exactly two minutes. I'm still amazed that we managed to get all the dogs into their costumes and they're all sitting patiently. It's like they know that they're part of something awesome and they're excited to be here.

"Yup!" I say.

Mrs. Paisley gives me a thumbs-up, which means it's time for me to go to the megaphone. My stomach gets all rumbly, and I can't believe I'm going to speak in front of every person and dog on Seagate. But even though I'm nervous, I can't wait to do it. I can't wait for Mr. Brookfield's amazing talent to be known by every person on this island.

"I'll be right back," I tell Claire, Calvin, Bennett, and Micayla. Claire and Micayla know what's happening, of course, and as soon as I make the announcement about Mr. Brookfield, I'm going to hop off the stage and join them.

I follow Mrs. Paisley onto the stage and she whispers, "You know what you're going to say?"

I nod. I tried to write it down but nothing seemed right, so I just decided to memorize some thoughts and then speak from my heart. I think I can do it.

"Welcome to Seagate Halloween!" Mrs. Paisley yells into the megaphone. "This has been a tradition for fifty years, but traditions can always be improved upon, as you will soon see. So I'm turning this over to Remy Boltuck, a Seagater since birth!"

"Hello, everyone," I say softly, and then realize I need to get people pumped up. "Hello, Seagate Island! The best place on earth!" I yell, and everyone starts cheering. "I know you're all as excited as I am for Seagate Halloween, so I don't want to take up too much time. But sometimes people have a secret talent that's really, really awesome, but no one knows about it. And then when one person finds out, she feels the need to tell everyone.

"So, without further ado, I'd like to bring out Mr. Donald Brookfield. I'm sure you've all seen him around—sitting on the bench by Dog Beach, sipping coffee at Mornings, and always ordering the butter pecan sundae at Sundae Best. But you didn't know he had this super amazing skill and that he's been in hundreds of movies—or at least, his voice has. So sit back, relax, put on your best listening ears, and enjoy the show!"

After that, everyone starts cheering even louder, and I wish that I could see Bennett's and Calvin's faces. I hand the megaphone back to Mrs. Paisley, and then Mr. Brookfield comes out—dressed exactly like Calvin in fancy jeans, spiked hair, and a popped-collar polo. It's so funny.

I run off the stage and catch up to the group right at the beginning of the parade route.

"I can't believe you did this, Rem," Bennett says, squeezing my hand for a second and then letting it go. "Claire and Micayla said this was all your idea."

I shrug. "They helped." I look up at the stage and see Mr. Brookfield about to start. "Shh. Listen."

"Welcome, Seagaters," Mr. Brookfield says in his spooky voice. "I dressed as my grandson Calvin Reich. He'll probably kill me for embarrassing him, but he's one of the best guys I know—so I had to do it." And then he pauses for a minute. Everyone looks around, wondering what's about to happen. Maybe he's quiet for more than a minute—I'm not sure, because my heart is pounding and I'm too excited. I know what's coming. I wonder what's spookier: knowing what's coming or not knowing what's coming. I guess that's true when it comes to Seagate Halloween and Mr. Brookfield's scream and life in general.

Finally, he does it.

He screams.

Aaaaheeeeoowwwww!

Mr. Brookfield's famous scream is broadcast all across Seagate. Everyone at the parade hears it, and I'm sure even latecomers on their way to the parade hear it.

Mr. Brookfield's scream is different from how it used to

be, different from the recording I'd heard so many times. It's scratchier, maybe. It sounds older. But that doesn't mean it sounds bad.

This scream is a link from Mr. Brookfield's past to his future and the start of the parade all at the same time. It's kind of like a link to my old life on Seagate and my new one too.

It takes people a few seconds to realize that they've heard that scream before. And that they've heard it recently. I watch the people in the crowd turn to one another and whisper, and I bet they're saying that it's the scream from the scary movies that have been shown the past few Sunday nights. They get so excited when they realize it—cheering and clapping—until finally all of Seagate is giving Mr. Brookfield a standing ovation.

"See?" I whisper to Claire. "He is a celebrity! A real-life celebrity!"

"I know! And it's the best thing ever!"

Our little doggie day care staff high-five one another, and then we all run to join Mr. Brookfield on the stage. Everyone is cheering, and one by one we approach the microphone and scream. Our own, individual screams. We try to mimic Mr. Brookfield's *Aaaaheeeeoowwwww*, but the screams are all our own.

Claire's is soft and high-pitched, with lots of laughter mixed in. Bennett's and Calvin's are loud and goofy. And Micayla's sounds more like a song than a scream. I don't know what mine is—nervous and excited sounding, I guess. It's almost shocking that this sound is coming out of my mouth.

There's more cheering and more screaming, and it feels like the whole island is a part of it. Everyone who is here now will remember it forever.

After the cheering dies down, I make my way to the microphone again.

"As if that wasn't awesome enough, we have something even more awesome for you! We're starting something new. The first annual Mr. Brookfield Seagate Scream Contest. After the Pooch Parade, everyone who wants to participate should find me on the stage and sign up. We'll have an hour to practice while everyone's enjoying their SGI Sweets, and then we'll have the contest."

Soon it's time for the Pooch Parade. This used to be everyone's favorite part of Seagate Halloween, but I have a feeling the Scream Contest will change that. And that's okay, I think. It's okay to have new favorites.

We make sure all the dogs are with us, and we start marching. We get so many cheers and hoots and "That's so cute" as we walk. The dogs are barking and strutting their stuff, and I can't tell who feels proudest right now—Calvin and Claire about Mr. Brookfield's awesome performance, the dogs for being such a fabulous part of the parade, or me for being surrounded by amazing dogs and amazing friends.

I've had so many perfect moments in all my years on Seagate Island. But this moment, right now, feels the most perfect.

It's not the past that matters so much, or even the future. It's right now.

Right now, the moment you're living, is really the most important.

The scream contest gets off to a chaotic start.
There's a line around the block of people who want to participate—mostly boys between the ages of eight and fourteen. But Calvin, Claire, Bennett, and Micayla help me collect the names. Next to us, Mr. Brookfield offers coaching, free of charge.

It feels like the whole island is milling about, everyone eating candy, chatting, and savoring the last days of summer on Seagate Island, the best place on earth.

I go up to the microphone one more time. I don't need everybody to pay attention, but I hope some people do. So all I say is, "Seagate Island, get ready to scream!" I tell all the contest participants to stay quiet while the others scream. I feel like a teacher, or maybe a camp counselor. I think these kids may be harder to control than the dogs!

Mr. Brookfield starts off the contest with his famous scream, and then one by one, the participants go to the microphone and say their name and then scream.

It's chaotic and crazy and hilarious and amazing all at the same time.

Mrs. Paisley looks like she has a headache, but she's smiling anyway.

Finally, after the last competitor screams, Mr. Brookfield announces that the judges will vote in the next few hours and the winners will be posted tomorrow.

And we get to be the judges!

Later that night, Mr. Brookfield invites us over for one last pizza party, and it's hard to believe that this is the last time we'll do this for a whole year. But tonight's pizza party is different. It's not just the six of us. There are seven others here: Oscar, Marilyn Monroe, Atticus, Rascal, Palm, Tabby, and Potato Salad.

The dog owners thought it was funny that their dogs were invited to Mr. Brookfield's house and they weren't. Mr. Brookfield's pretty famous now, so they're a little jealous. But the dogs are part of our crew. They can't be left out on our last night.

The dogs sit at our feet and run around the backyard as we eat our pizza. We chat, reminisce about the summer, and talk about what the coming year will be like. Micayla promises that she'll email us every day to tell us about year-round life on Seagate. Calvin and Claire promise that they'll be back next summer.

"I can't believe we waited so long to spend a summer here," Claire says.

Calvin adds, "Yeah, and we had to be forced to do it."

"And just think," I say, "if you had played tennis at tennis camp, you might never have come back, Claire." I smile at her, and she smiles back and then hits me on the arm.

"You're never going to let that go, huh?"

"Nope!"

"If only Mason Redmond were here," Bennett says, in his jokey way, looking at Micayla and rubbing Potato Salad's belly. "Then the summer would be complete. It's a shame he had to leave early. Was he taking the SATs or something?"

Micayla rolls her eyes, and at just that moment Marilyn Monroe hops up onto her lap.

"Oh, leave her alone," Claire says. "Maybe you should be—"

"Should be what?" Bennett asks.

Claire looks at me. I speak to her in blinks, urging her not to embarrass me, not to ruin this most perfect day. She giggles a little. I wait for her to say something else. I mentally plead with her to change the subject.

"Maybe you should be a forward thinker," she says, shrugging, like it's no big deal, like it's what she planned to say all along. "Mason's not so bad. Leave Micayla alone."

Phew! Good cover-up. For once she didn't say the most embarrassing thing she could think of.

"Wow. Claire Reich, suddenly the one who's looking out for everyone." Bennett nods like he totally approves. "Anyone who looks out for Micayla is a friend of mine." He high-fives her, and then slowly and nonchalantly Claire winks at me.

As we finish our pizza, I tell them that I have an announcement to make, and I grab Marilyn Monroe from Micayla. "Marilyn Monroe and I are becoming roommates soon," I say. "Actually, next week!"

"Huh?" Micayla asks.

So I tell them the whole story about Amber and Marilyn Monroe and the new apartment and everything.

"Will your parents say yes?" Claire asks.

"Yeah, I asked them, and they said yes right away. I couldn't believe it, but then they said how impressed they were with the dog-sitting business, and how responsible I have been."

"You didn't say anything to him, did you?" Claire asks me a few minutes later, when Bennett and Calvin are attempting to play Ping-Pong in the air, without a table.

"What?" I ask, confused, still thinking about what it will be like when Marilyn Monroe is my dog. Really and truly my dog.

"About how you feel," she whispers, talking through her teeth. "Bennett."

I shake my head.

"How come?"

"I didn't feel the need to. Things are so great right now. I know that things change, and pretty often it's great when they do," I tell her. "But in this moment, for now, I just want this one thing to stay the same. I'm happy now, and I'm scared to think about things with Bennett and me being that different. Know what I mean?"

Claire nods. "I do."

"And besides," I say and put my arm around her, "there's always next summer."

We sit around talking for a while longer, and as we're talking, I look around at my old friends and my new friends, my human friends and my dog friends, and I realize that this summer and especially Seagate Halloween were completely different from all the ones that came before. Different and sometimes scary and hard.

But they were also better. Better than I could have ever imagined.

ACKNOWLEDGMENTS

First and foremost, I owe an ocean of gratitude to Aleah Violet Rosenberg and her amazing napping skills. Without them, this book would have never been written.

Thanks to Dave for all of the ideas, love, and support. And thanks for indulging my beach house dreams. One day, it will happen.

Thank you, Mom and Dad, for finally getting me a dog when I was in ninth grade, and for everything else, too.

David and Max, thanks for taking Yoffi out all those times when I was feeling lazy. You're superhero brothers and two of my best friends.

Thanks to Bubbie and Zeyda for being dog lovers, for introducing me to my first dog love, Candy, and for being wonderful in every way.

To the Rosenberg family—Karen, Aaron, Elon, Justin, Ari,

Ezra, Maayan, Libby, Bruce, Debbie, Marty, and Donna—thanks for all the encouragement and enthusiasm and for being "dog people."

Many thanks to Arthur, the Franks, the Freels, the Hermans, the Rosensteins, and the Friedmans. I feel the love all the way from Indiana.

Oodles of thanks to the Sterns and the Lincers and all the dog stories you've shared.

Thanks to Tata, Beard, Sarah, Aaron, and Juju for sharing your magical Block Island house with me and for providing me with so much inspiration for this story.

Caroline, Jenny, and Siobhan, thanks for all the help, the writing retreats, and the laughter.

Hugs and kisses and so much appreciation for Rhonda, Melanie, Margaret Ann, and the whole BWL family.

Alyssa Eisner Henkin, I say this every time because it's true: You're the best agent in the world, and I owe you everything. You can come stay at my beach house anytime.

A whole sea of thanks goes to Howard, Steve, Susan, Jason, Chad, Maria, Jessie, Jen, Meagan, Nicole, Laura, Elisa, and everyone at Abrams and Amulet. Thank you, thank you, thank you!

Maggie Lehrman, thanks for believing in this book and for being as excited about it as I am. You've made every page better than I could have imagined. There will be an Adirondack chair on the front porch waiting for you.

THE STORY CONTINUES IN *DOG BEACH UNLEASHED*, THE SEQUEL TO *WELCOME TO DOG BEACH*. READ THE FIRST CHAPTER NOW!

Dog Beach Unleashed

This is it. This moment. My favorite moment of the entire year.

I'm sitting in one of the movie-theater-like seats on the ferry. On the top level, of course. I watch the mainland disappear behind me, and then all I see is ocean. Ocean and ocean and ocean. And it feels like forever until I'll get there. *Hurry up*, I think. But then I change my mind. Don't hurry up. Let me enjoy this. Enjoy the almost there.

But then, little by little, I start to see it—bits and pieces of Seagate Island. I see the lighthouse and then the bright orange cottage that sits right on the shoreline. And I get closer. Closer and closer. And I see more things take shape.

My heart is flopping with excitement, like a caught fish that's about to get back into the water.

My mom is on one side of me, my dad on the other. Marilyn Monroe is on my lap. The whole summer is spread out in front of me like a big picnic blanket on the sand.

And this summer isn't like any other summer. This is Seagate's centennial summer. One hundred years since the first person came to Seagate. One hundred years of pink sunsets and Sundae Best's overflowing ice cream cups. One hundred years of flip-flops click-clacking on the boardwalk. One hundred years of Ping-Pong tournaments and summertime friends—some of the best friends in the world.

There's going to be a huge party—Seagate Island's birthday party—for everyone to celebrate together. Carnival rides. A photo booth. A talent show. Mrs. Pursuit volunteered to be in charge of the celebration committee. They've been planning it since last summer.

"I just got a text from Vivian." My mom taps my knee. "They took the earlier ferry."

I nod. "Oh. Okay."

Vivian Newhouse is Bennett's mom and one of my mom's best friends. They've known each other since Bennett and I were newborn babies. That's when Bennett and I met, too, although, obviously, I can't remember that meeting. He's one of those people who's always been there. There's never been a time when I didn't know Bennett Newhouse.

Bennett had texted me that they were taking the noon ferry, just like us. I looked for him everywhere but couldn't find him. Now I know why.

I wonder if Bennett will be waiting when we get there,

standing at the ferry terminal, looking for us as we come off the boat.

I haven't seen him in a whole year, and when I think about him, all I can picture is what he looked like at the end of last summer—shaggy hair, cargo shorts with holes in them, pizza-stained T-shirts. I'm sure he's gotten taller. Maybe he'll even be wearing new summer clothes. They won't be torn or stained. They'll look crisp, the tags just cut off. Everything fresh for a new summer.

I thought about Bennett this whole year. We e-mailed a lot and talked on the phone. But none of that's the same as being with him in person.

I flip-flopped back and forth all year long. Did I like him as more than a friend? Sometimes I thought I did. And some-times I thought I didn't. I kept telling myself that I'd figure it out on Seagate. Things always seem clearer there. Every-thing makes more sense when you're near the ocean.

But there's one conversation we had that lingers in the back of my mind.

We were on the phone one Saturday night. It was Feb-ruary, the month when the past summer feels like a million years ago, and the next summer feels like a million years away.

It was after ten at night, and I'm never supposed to be on the phone that late. But my parents were out, and I'd told the babysitter I was going to bed. Which I was. But then Bennett called. And we were talking. Mostly about stupid stuff, like this crazy new burrito he'd tried, and the fact that people camp outside certain stores so they can be the first ones to get the new sneakers. But then he brought up first kisses. Something about this girl Mara who keeps a list of who in the grade has kissed someone and who hasn't.

"You haven't kissed anyone yet, right?" he asked me.

I stayed quiet, but then I said that no, I hadn't.

And he said he hadn't, either.

"Oh," I said.

"We could be each other's first kiss," he said, as if it were no big deal. As if he were saying we could play Ping-Pong or we could share a chocolate croissant or we could sit on his dock and throw pebbles into the ocean.

My heart thumped in my chest. And I said, "Sure."

But even as I was saying it, I was thinking that I wasn't sure I wanted that to happen. I told myself that even if it did happen, summer was so far away that I didn't need to worry about it or even think about it.

It was something I could deal with later.

I pushed the thought away. As far away as possible.

But that later is now quickly approaching. That far away is getting so much closer.

We'll be together for a whole summer. And I know I said *sure,* but now I don't know if I want to.

I look out the ferry window. We're almost there.

I keep thinking the same thing: Will I see him as Bennett, the same old Bennett I've always known? Or will I see him as something more? The way I saw him at the end of last summer.

A whole year has passed. Are we different now?

As much as I don't want to be different, I think I am. As much as I want everything to always stay the same, I know that things change. And I know that change can be okay, that I can handle it. *Sometimes*, anyway.

But the one thing I can't handle is the not knowing. I always want to know how things are going to work out.

When I start a book, I skip ahead and read the last page first. Always. I don't read mysteries. I hate surprise parties.

Marilyn Monroe smiles her gentle Yorkie smile. She looks up at me and licks my chin, as if she senses I can use some reassuring. I wonder if she knows where we're going. I've told her a million times. I even showed her the countdown calendar I had on my computer and the real, paper calendar I had hanging above my desk, with all the days that had been X-ed off in red marker.

"We're almost there, Mari," I whisper. Her ears perk up, and she shuffles on my lap. "Sit, sit. A little while longer."

"So, all your clients know you're coming back?" my dad asks me. "Do you need to have an orientation for the dogs? Get them ready for camp or anything?"

I smile. "That's a good idea, actually. Maybe we should have some kind of easing-in process, like I had for preschool and kindergarten?"

Everyone needs time to get situated, to warm up. Even

dogs. Life is like a freezing-cold pool that way. We all need to dip a toe before we jump in.

"Good thinking, Rem." My mom pats my leg, and I wonder if she's as excited as I am. She's been coming to Seagate Island for over forty years now, since her own childhood. I wonder if this amazing anticipation ever fades. After year twenty do you start to get used to it?

I want to ask her, but what if the answer's yes? That it's not as exciting as it used to be? If it is, I don't want to know.

ABOUT THE AUTHOR

Lisa Greenwald is the author of *Reel Life Starring Us*, *Sweet Treats & Secret Crushes*, and the Pink & Green series. She works in the library at the Birch Wathen Lenox School in Manhattan. She is a graduate of the New School's MFA program in writing for children and lives in Brooklyn. Visit her online at lisagreenwald.com.

CHECK OUT THESE OTHER GREAT READS FROM LISA GREENWALD!

FROM THE AUTHOR OF *MY LIFE IN PINK & GREEN*

LISA GREENWALD

Reel Life
STARRING US

FROM THE AUTHOR OF *MY LIFE IN PINK & GREEN*

LISA GREENWALD

Sweet Treats & Secret Crushes

My Life in Pink & Green

LISA GREENWALD

My Summer of
Pink & Green

LISA GREENWALD

THE THIRD BOOK IN THE *PINK & GREEN* SERIES
Pink & Green
IS THE
NEW BLACK
LISA GREENWALD